T0146620

LUST AND REDEMPTION

LUST AND REDEMPTION

A Miss Mary Margaret Story

Book III

Mary Frances Hodges

Lust and Redemption
A MISS MARY MARGARET STORY

iUniverse books may be ordered through booksellers or by contacting:

iUniverse
1663 Liberty Drive
Bloomington, IN 47403
www.iuniverse.com
1-800-Authors (1-800-288-4677)

ISBN: 978-1-5320-6552-1 (sc)
ISBN: 978-1-5320-6554-5 (hc)
ISBN: 978-1-5320-6553-8 (e)

Library of Congress Control Number: 2019900468

Print information available on the last page.

iUniverse rev. date: 01/14/2019

I appreciate my cousin, and fellow writer, Joe Harwell for his assistance with this book.

Contents

CHAPTER ONE

The Return

It seemed strange and yet so familiar. Harris felt as if he were about to walk into a previous life, which in a sense he was. The doorman opened the heavy oak door at Alfred's and greeted him with, "Mr. McGinty, welcome back. It's good to see you. The Harwells are already here, and they are expecting you."

The supper club was filled with people, and everyone was as festive as ever-just as he remembered it. "Harris, we are over here." Maggie Harwell rose and hugged him when he got to the table. "Harris, I thought I'd never see you again. Her eyes filled with tears. Harris kissed Maggie on the check. Harris was a man who always stood out in a crowd. He was just over six feet tall, with a head full of curly, black hair, and big blue eyes which told of his Irish heritage even before you heard his last name.

Everyone around the table greeted him warmly. They were genuinely glad to see him. The champagne was already flowing adding to the ambience of mirth and well-being. *"Fuss and feathers"* was the thought that went though Harris' mind. *"Vanity, all is Vanity"*.

Ross Adams, who was well into his cups, asked in too loud a voice, "Harris, did they let you out, or did you escape?"

Harris answered; "I've come back to Denver for two months to test my vocation. Father Abbott wanted me to make sure I want the monastic life, before I start taking vows."

"Oh, well good then," Ross continued," We have time to get you to forget about that nonsense, and see the light about staying in Denver. I bet you spend a lot of time saying those beads."

"That's quite enough, Ross," said Tom Harwell.

"Just another uninformed Protestant," thought Harris.

Several waiters appeared with trays loaded with food. Harris was glad something had distracted Ross, but he wasn't used to such rich food: Prime roast beef, potatoes lyonnaise, and fried egg plant were certainly different from the simple fare he had eaten at the monastery. Harris wasn't sure his stomach was up to such cuisine, and definitely not the tray of appetizers full of various types of olives and baked squares of flakey dough stuffed with spinach and artichoke hearts.

"Eat up," Tom said to Harris, it sounded almost like a command. "You have lost a lot of weight in the past ten months."

"Do you plan to go back, and stay?" asked Horace Tabor.

"Yes," Harris said. "If they will have me."

"You are really serious about going back, aren't you?" asked Horace

"Yes, I am very serious."

"Tell us what you have been doing since you've been home?" asked Emily Smith, who was also a Catholic, and sensed Harris' discomfort.

"I go to Mass every morning, and then stay for instruction

and discussion with Father Sullivan. And I spend a great deal of time in thought and prayer."

"Enough of this," chided Maggie. "Let the boy eat his supper. This is a party and not an interrogation."

Everyone changed the subject, but Harris turned a deaf ear to the gossip. *"Christ, can't they think of anything better to talk about?"* thought Harris.

Harris' eyes glanced over the entire dining room and he knew most of the people there. Many of them smiled at him, and he smiled back. He noticed a young woman with raven black hair in a yellow evening gown at one of the tables. He had no idea who she was, maybe someone's guest. Alfred's is a very exclusive supper club, and you couldn't come here unless you were a patron or the guest of a member. Harris felt his member starting to react to her beauty, but he quickly looked away. The Brothers at the monastery had cautioned him this might happen. They were men first, and monks second. He shouldn't be alarmed, they had cautioned.

Following dessert, Tom invited Harris to join him on the side porch for a cigar. Harris gladly accepted, although he didn't know how he would react to the cigar. Not like before, when he was almost never without a cigar. He could have smoked at the monastery, but cigars were considered a luxury. To Harris, the atmosphere of the dining room at Alfred's was smothering.

When they got outside, Tom said, "How is it going, really?"

"It's certainly different from what I have been experiencing, I'm trying to get my legs back under me again."

"Have you been to her grave yet?"

"Yes, and it was hard, but I did all right."

Tom said, "I was going to go with you if you hadn't"

"Next week, I plan to come see Annie. I'm trying to take everything a step at a time." said Harris.

"She's grown so much, she's hardly a baby anymore," commented Tom.

"I'm ashamed to say I don't even remember what she looks like."

"How could you, everything considered? She favors Sophie," Tom said.

"I'm glad."

"Harris, you entered the monastery under duress, now that time has passed, do you really think you will be happy there the rest of your life?"

"I really liked it there, I have grown to love the rhythm of the monastic life. Being there, brought back a lot of happy memories of being raised by the clergy and the nuns. I suppose it was like returning to the womb. I think I will be happy there. That's why I am home for two months to see if I really want to go back of my own accord."

"I'm not going to do anything to dissuade you from returning, if that is really what you are meant to do" said Tom.

Tom's wife, Mary Margaret, who had always gone by Maggie, was the energy source that kept Tom going. He adored her. Few people knew that she was his second wife. Even on the frontier, divorce was not acceptable to most people.

Maggie stood only five feet four, but her presence was felt by everyone around her. She was loved by her friends and those who were acquaintances, admired her. The faint pink color on her cheeks told of an English heritage. Her age was a closely guarded secret. She always lied to the census takers about her age. She looked at least ten years younger than her actual age, and she was fifteen years younger than Tom. She believed her age was none of the business of the U.S. government. Maggie fashioned her waist length brown hair into braids and wrapped them around the top of her head like a coronet, which was a telltale sign of a more recent Southern influence.

"Tom, who is the woman in the yellow dress at Mrs. Alford's table?" Harris asked. "I think I know everyone here, but her. I don't remember ever seeing her before."

"That's the Widow King," replied Tom. "Her husband dropped dead quite unexpectedly about three years ago. He owned the Abel Sheep Ranch. They didn't come into town much. I don't ever remember seeing them here at Alfred's"

"A-b-e-l, as in the first herdsman in the Bible?" asked Harris.

"Yes."

"Who bought the ranch after he died?"

"No one, she never put it up for sale," remarked Tom.

"She runs it by herself?"

"Yes, but she has good help. Carlos Ayala is the chief shepherd, and they swear he does know the name of every sheep in the permanent holding pen. It's a large spread, about a thousand acres."

Harris showed shock and amazement as he listened.

"You can ask anybody, though, and they will tell you that Kathleen is the boss. She's done a very good job of making the ranch even more profitable. I know because I am on the bank's board of Directors. Would you like to meet her?"

"Good Lord, no! I was just curious as to who she was."

Three nights later Harris returned to Alfred's for dinner. It was Friday, and that night the main entrée would be baked salmon with caper butter sauce. That salmon made giving up meat on Fridays, worth it. Harris had never considered salmon much of a sacrifice, but he wasn't one to argue. On many Fridays at the monastery some of the brothers would go down to the Brazos River and catch enough trout for everyone's supper. Harris liked baked trout, but they were nothing compared to salmon at Alfred's.

All the "blue bloods" were there at Alfred's. That was his nickname for his friends. Harris grew up in an orphanage. Although he knew only a few details about his parents, he knew enough to know they were not among the upper crust. He had been well educated and well-traveled, thanks to a mysterious trust fund, so he fit in with all sorts of people. Harris was well liked by his friends.

The salmon was as delicious as he remembered, and he allowed himself to have one of Alfred's chocolate mousses which everyone agreed was sinful in itself. So much for overindulgence! He wasn't apt to see such a dessert at the monastery and didn't know how many more Fridays he would stay in Denver.

There she was again, beautiful as ever. She had on a pale blue dress, which made her blue eyes look even larger. *"Well, what the Hell!"* Harris then asked Tom to introduce the Widow King to him. Tom arched one eyebrow and said, "Of course."

They approached what was called, by the locals, the widow's table, and after greeting the other older ladies. at the table, Tom introduced Kathleen King to Harris.

"It's a pleasure to meet you." Harris lifted her hand and kissed it, much to Kathleen's surprise. Then he asked if she cared to dance. In addition to serving the best cuisine in Denver, Alfred's had a small orchestra and a medium size dance floor. The orchestra played every Friday and Saturday night.

Harris led Kathleen to the dance floor, and all the chattering in the room stopped. He was so thankful it was a waltz so he didn't have to hold her tight. They both would have been embarrassed. At the end of the dance, he escorted her back to her table, and there was light applause from the other patrons. There were many reasons why people might have applauded, but he wasn't going to clutter his mind thinking about them.

After she was seated, he leaned in and said, "I have two tickets to Jenny Lend's fifth farewell performance tomorrow night. Would you do me the honor of accompanying me?"

"Why, yes. That would be delightful," she replied.

"Wonderful, I will come for you at seven, if that is good for you?"

She responded, "Of course."

Harris started away from the table, and then turned around and said, "I don't know where you live." It had been an unplanned remark, but it worked out well. "So why don't I take you home tonight, so I'll know. Whenever you are ready to leave, let me know. Now would be just fine, unless you wish to stay later," said Harris.

"Now would be fine," was her reply.

Harris helped her with her light shawl. Even in the summers in Denver, it is cool at night. Every pair of eyes in the place followed the couple as they left.

Maggie looked quizzically at Tom who just shrugged his shoulders.

When they arrived at Kathleen's house, he escorted her to

the front door, once again kissed her hand and said that he looked forward to tomorrow night.

Kathleen entered the parlor and Maria, her housekeeper and best friend, came around the corner from the kitchen area. Kathleen slapped both hands over her mouth, and then said, "Oh, Maria! I have just met the most handsome man."

Maria grinned and said, "It's about time. We have all prayed you would meet someone and fall in love."

"You all have prayed about it? Why?"

"Why?" Marria repeated the question. "Because, we know you are lonely, and you are too young not to have any happiness in your life."

Kathleen hugged her. "What would I do without my Mexican family?"

Maria was the porotype of a middle-aged Mexican woman. She was short and had a full figure from too many babies and too starchy a diet. Her black hair had yet to gray.

Harris had a very fitful sleep. He was so attracted to Kathleen, but he had promised himself to go back to the monastery and take his vows. He wanted to study to be a priest. But Kathleen was so beautiful and had such a lovely figure. Apparently the Devil was after him. The Jesuits would say that Kathleen was placed in his path to test whether or not he was serious about becoming a monk/priest. Harris was rapidly failing that test.

The next morning after Mass, Harris entered Tom's mining office and was braced for the questions that were sure to follow. "Well, confession didn't take long this morning," quipped Tom.

"There was nothing to confess, that concerns you," retorted Harris.

"Are you going to see her again?"

"Yes, we are going to the Jenny Lend performance. Will you and Maggie be there?"

"No, we've been to several of her final performances. We are going to pass up this one."

CHAPTER TWO

Do I Stay, or do I go?

Harris arrived promptly at seven and Kathleen had on a lavender suit with a white blouse covered with tiny violets. Once again he was overwhelmed at her beauty. There was no way for her to know that violets were his favorite flower. After the performance, they went to Griffin's Ice Cream Parlor which was a new, novel feature to Denver's attractions. They ate ice cream and chatted, and Harris silently thought about the times the monks made ice cream-mostly vanilla. Sometimes just ice cream made of snow. Those were happy memories.

When they arrived at Kathleen's house, she invited him in, and he didn't hesitate to accept. They sat on couches facing each other before the fire place. Maria served them tea. Then suddenly Harris got up and moved over to Kathleen's couch, sat down, took her in his arms, and kissed her. She was surprised, but not displeased.

"I'm sorry if I offended you. I should have asked first."

"You didn't ask; but I quite enjoyed it," replied Kathleen."

"May I kiss you again?"

"Yes, and you don't need to keep asking."

Harris wrapped his arms around her, held her tightly and eagerly kissed her on her mouth, and she just as eagerly returned the kisses. It was as if they couldn't get enough of each other.

When neither could breathe, they stopped and laughed. Kathleen said, "I guess we have both been wanting to do that."

Harris thought, *"I would like to do more. I either have to leave or rape her. I have never forced a woman and certainly won't start with Kathleen."*

"I really must go," Harris said reluctantly.

"Oh, stay, stay please stay," Kathleen thought.

He kissed her again and then led her to the door where he kissed her quite firmly. "May I see you tomorrow?"

"Yes, why don't I have Maria pack us a picnic lunch. I know a nice plateau not too far out, and with a spyglass you can see my ranch from there."

"Wonderful, would ten o'clock be a good time for you."

"I'll be ready then."

Harris brushed her lips with his and then walked down the steps to his buggy. He was in great need of a release and had two choices. He could visit the Lovely Rachel at Miss Laura's, but so many new men from all over the country were flooding into Denver, carrying who knows what diseases with them. There was no way he was going to risk transferring one of those to Kathleen. He realized then he planned to do more than just kiss her. The other choice was to go home and indulge himself in self-abuse, or so the Church called it.

He decided on the latter. It would just be something else to confess. He had to do something to release the pressure. It had been a long time since he had had to masturbate. He had been married, and before he came back to the Catholic Church, he had visited the Lovely Rachel two or three times a week. She was always delighted to see him, she said he was her favorite customer. Plus member-wise he had the most to offer. His size had always been a blessing and a curse.

Ruis knocked on the door to signal the nightly champagne was ready. Harris considered not even bothering with the sparkling wine. He was sure he would sleep soundly that night; and he did have the best night of sleep since returning from Pecos. After the first month at the monastery, the nightly emission had stopped, and since he was determined to become celebrate he dismissed any thought of using self-abuse to calm his nerves. Lord, he had had too much to confess when he got there to add even one more thing to the list.

The next morning Harris arrived at ten as promised. Maria had packed a picnic basket with thick ham and roast beef sandwiches, both on Maria's homemade bread. There were hard boiled eggs, a small lemon pound cake, and a bottle of red wine. Maria had included a checkered tablecloth and matching napkins and the necessary eating utensils.

Kathleen had noticed that Harris' buggy was very fancy and extremely well made. The two chestnut colored horses were from a good blood line. She didn't know a lot about horses, but she could recognize the product of a good blood line. She thought originally he must have borrowed the buggy and horses from the Harwells to impress her. It was really a very fine outfit for an accountant. Today, these apparently were his own. Maybe his wife, who died, left him a lot of money. She directed him how to get to her favorite picnic place. It's a large ledge that juts out from one of the many mountains in that area. The cliff above it still had trees growing along the edge and gave ample shade to the ledge below.

"Would you like to see my ranch?" she asked.

"Of course." He took her hand and he guided her through the large rocks and scrub brush to the edge of the cliff. She pulled out a spyglass and pointed it to the northeast and handed it to him.

"It's there in the distance." Harris squinted his eye and finally focused on a large adobe and log house, and beyond that what appeared to be a collection of smaller housing units. Even farther away from the main house there was a myriad of pens. The pens seemed to be empty.

"Where are the sheep?"

"They are in the high meadows until the end of August. Sooner if the weather starts moving in. That's why I get to be in town this summer as there is little for me to do at the ranch. Since my aunt died, and left me the house in town, I decided to take advantage of city life."

"No sheep at all?"

"Yes, a few weaker lambs and some pet ones are kept behind to help entertain the children."

"How many people live at your ranch?"

"About thirty. They are all employees. They aren't slaves, and can come and go as they please. Two of Carlos and Maria's sons and their families live and work on the ranch. Sometimes one or two of the young men will spread their wings and leave for a year or two, but they usually come back."

Kathleen focused her attention on him and said, "I'm hungry, how about you?"

"I'd like dessert first," replied Harris.

"Oh?" And he kissed her tenderly. "I'd like some dessert later, I believe," she said and giggled.

"That can be arranged," he said with a big grin on his face." He thought, *"I hope it will be a lot more than kissing."*

She spread the tablecloth and the food. Harris opened the wine and filled the two glasses Maria had included. He cut the cake and said, "Here, let me feed you." She opened her mouth as if she were a baby bird waiting to be fed. He placed a small piece into her mouth and followed it with a soft kiss.

"Oh, you are tricky, Mr. McGinty."

"Would you like some more cake?" he asked.

"Hmm. Lemon pound cake never tasted so good."

She gathered up the remains of the lunch and the tablecloth and forks and placed them in the basket. Harris retrieved a quilt and two small pillows from the buggy.

He said, "I think we should let our lunch settle." She had no objection. They lay there hand in hand watching clouds against that incredibly blue Colorado sky and described what animal or plant each cloud looked like. They laughed while doing that, obviously enjoying each other's company.

Harris turned onto his side and leaned over and kissed her. "I would like to make love to you," he said.

"I think I would like for you to." Fred had been such a terror in bed. She sensed that Harris would be completely different although she was a little nervous about it.

He took off his pants and was reaching for a French Letter when she said, "That's not necessary. I'm barren."

Are you sure?" asked Harris.

"Dr. Murphy said I am," she responded.

"If Dr. Murphy said so, it's true," Harris stated. "He knows everything about everybody in town, but all he ever talks about is the weather and whether or not his steak is cooked properly."

Kathleen had raised her long skirts up to her waist line. Harris noticed that other than the layers of petticoats she didn't have on any undergarments. Maybe she had counted on this happening.

He kissed her eagerly, and she returned his kiss the same way. He started slipping his tongue into her mouth and she jerked back, eyes wide. "I was just going to give you a French Kiss."

"I don't know what that is."

He thought, *"She's been married before? Everyone knows that is upper persuasion for lower invasion."*

"I don't have to kiss you that way if you object. I was going to put my tongue into your mouth." He continued kissing her without any tongue being involved. He cupped her breasts in his hands, and she smiled at him, and seemed pleased. He sensed she was ready. She was more than ready. He entered her gently but did not fully insert because of the size of his member. He did not want to frighten her.

He had found only one woman who could take his member completely, and it was a whore in France. He very slowly moved in and out of her, kissing her continually and found his tongue in her mouth without realizing he had done so. She did seem to instinctively know what to do. It was over too soon for both of them. He rolled to the side. and she was sobbing.

"Oh, Lord, did I hurt you?" Harris asked.

"No," but she sobbed and kept sobbing.

"What's wrong?"

"It was wonderful. It was what I always thought married love should be like."

He kissed away her tears, but was at a loss for words. Finally he said, "I'm glad I pleased you."

"You have no idea how much you pleased me," she whispered.

"Would you like for me to please you again?"

"Right now, you mean, now?" she inquired eagerly.

"Well, whenever you like."

"I'd like it right now," she said smiling.

She had been a widow for three years and her need must have been as great as his, he concluded. He was never one to turn down such an invitation, and he wanted more than anything to give this woman pleasure.

Harris entered her again, and this time put his hands on each side of her hips and motioned for her to move them. She had lay perfectly still the first time. She soon realized what he was asking her to do and she complied readily.

Once again she was crying when it was over. "Kathleen, are you all right? Have I done something wrong."

"No, you did everything right. I never had Fred make love to me that way. You were wonderful."

Harris let out a sigh of relief. He held her close to him until her tears stopped.

Finally he said, "I would love nothing better than to stay here with you, but we are burning daylight. We need to be able to see our way home."

She got up, dropped the hems of her skirts to the ground,

and smiled at him. "Thank you for the best afternoon of my life."

"It was truly my pleasure," was his reply. He offered her his hand to help her up into the buggy. They rode home in silence, holding hands.

He saw her to the door, squeezed her hand, and said, "I'll see you at 7:30"

Kathleen went inside. She set down the picnic basket and said, "Oh, Maria. I am a fallen woman."

"Thank God! It's about time," exclaimed Maria.

"But what we did was a sin." said Kathleen.

"Did he force you?"

"Never!"

"Did you enjoy it?"

"Oh yes, it was like a wonderful dream," said Kathleen.

"Then it was no sin," Maria said flatly. "You go lie down and rest. You know he is going to want more of that tonight. You must get into the bathtub to let your lady parts soak. I'll get a bath ready for you. You'll want to be fresh for him over your entire body"

"Oh, I should be so ashamed, but I am not."

They had already make plans to go to Alfred's for dinner. Harris arrived a little early which was somewhat unusual for him, but Kathleen was early, waiting for his arrival. Maria opened the door and once again when Kathleen entered the room he gasped at her beauty.

"I have a little something for you," he said smiling. He handed her a velvet rectangular box.

She looked puzzled, but then opened and exclaimed, "This is beautiful beyond words."

The box held an exquisite silver necklace with a sapphire drop and two small diamonds on each side of the sapphire.

"But if you are giving this to me, I can't accept it."

"Why?"

"Because it is too expensive. If you thought because of the events of the afternoon that you had to…"

"I most certainly did not," Harris protested.

"It's just too expensive." She was thinking, *"He's only an accountant. How can he afford this?"* She continued, "But how did you know what color dress I would be wearing tonight?"

"I had Ruis ask Maria."

"Then you didn't just randomly pick out this piece of jewelry because you knew my dress was sapphire color."

"No, I bought it to match your dress." The dress had a small scoop neckline which really showed off the necklace.

"Harris, this is really beautiful but I can't accept it," Kathleen protested again.

"Look, Jacque, who owns the jewelry store assured me if you didn't like it, I could bring it back in the morning," lied Harris.

"It's not that I don't like it. It is too expensive a gift for you to give me. He really said he would take it back?" quizzed Kathleen.

"Yes, I am a good customer…or at least I used to be."

That remark puzzled Kathleen.

"Will you please wear it for me tonight?"

She sighed, "All right, if you promise to take it back."

Avoiding giving her a promise, he said, "Please turn around

so I can clasp it around your neck. There. Now we are ready to go."

"Oooh, Miss Kathleen, you look so beautiful," said Maria as she handed her a wrap. Harris put his arm around Kathleen's waist and guided her out the door. He took her hand to help her into the carriage. As they were leaving, Harris slightly turned his head, and winked at Maria, who then crossed herself.

"I noticed you always sit at the Harwells table, will there be enough room for us there?"

"Oh yes, I own two of the seats at that table. We will always have a place to sit."

As they entered, Maggie Harwell called to Kathleen, "Come sit by me."

"Go ahead," Harris said. Although he had misgivings about Kathleen sitting by Maggie. "I'll sit across the table from you so I can see you better. You are so beautiful."

Kathleen blushed.

Maggie gushed, "Kathleen, you look absolutely fabulous tonight. Your necklace is outstanding."

Kathleen blushed again and said, "Thank you, but I am just wearing the necklace this evening."

"Why just this evening?" Maggie asked.

"It's too expensive a gift, but Harris said that Jacque would take it back in the morning."

"Harris actually said that to you," quizzed Maggie.

"Yes, ma'am."

"Sweet child, Harris has no intention of returning that gorgeous piece of jewelry. He gave it to you because he wanted you to have it. It matches your dress perfectly."

"I know but"…Kathleen protested.

Maggie placed her hand on top of Kathleen's and looked directly into her eyes. "Stop worrying about what the necklace cost. Harris has plenty of money. If he should go back to the monastery, which I thoroughly doubt now that he has met you, but if he does, you will still have that necklace. There are a dozen girls in Denver who would love to have Harris pay attention to them, with or without, a necklace. He is a very good lover in case you don't know"-then Maggie caught herself, and said, "at least that's what the rumor on the street is."

Kathleen was a little taken back at Maggie's bluntness, but said nothing. If the waiter hadn't refilled her wine glass immediately she would have done it herself. The waiters at Alfred's are trained to be attentive to their customers, and the young man serving their table must have picked up on the fact Kathleen was a little flustered. In fact, he always kept her wine glass full that night.

"Oh, mercy!" exclaimed Maggie, "The main entrée tonight is a leg of lamb in a cherry glaze."

"There's no problem with that," insisted Kathleen. "The lamb may be from my ranch actually. We do sell to Alfred's. I have no trouble eating lamb. It's a delicious meat. I would never knowingly eat lamb or mutton from my permanent flock, but as long as I did not know its name I'd have no trouble."

"You know your sheep by name?" Maggie asked incredulously.

"No, I know some of them by name, but Carlos, my chief herdsman, can tell each one of them apart, and their names, and which ones are their offspring. That's the sheep in the permanent flock that we keep exclusively for their wool and breeding purposes."

Maggie realized Kathleen could be plain spoken when it came to sheep, too.

The food arrived none too soon, the wine was really having an effect on Kathleen, and Harris watched from across the table and smiled quietly to himself. His girl could sure stand her own against Maggie. His stomach had knotted when Maggie insisted Kathleen sit by her.

When the ladies went to the powder room, Harris and Tom took cigars, and went to the side porch to talk, as much as anything.

"Is this a final fling before you go back?" Tom questioned.

"I don't know what it is? She is so beautiful. I am being tempted more ways than one." confessed Harris.

"Whatever your decision, we'll back you," said Tom.

"If I go back, will you rear Annie?" asked Harris.

"You know we will. Maggie is sure Tommy is about to take his first steps. Then it won't be much longer before Annie takes off walking. That will be exciting to see"

"I'll just have to see how things go with Kathleen. She does love that ranch. Going back to the monastery is something like going back to my original home. It's very comforting," said Harris.

When the evening was over, Harris asked Kathleen if she would like to go for a swim.

"A swim? Where on earth would you go for a swim in Denver?"

"At my house."

"You can't possibly be serious" Kathleen said in disbelief.

"No, I am very serious. I have a swimming pool."

"How can you? Your house is built almost on the side of a hill."

"It's an engineering feat, all right. I graduated with a degree in Engineering from Notre Dame. There's only one problem with my swimming pool."

"Oh," said Kaleen.

"No one is allowed to wear swimming outfits in the pool. One has to swim au natural, just as God made us in the womb."

Kathleen was quiet for a while and then said, "I haven't been swimming, since I was a girl in San Francisco. I wonder if I still know how? I only swam in the ocean."

Harris' mind went immediately to the south of France and struggled to erase the memory.

"I'll teach you. I think swimming comes naturally, so I imagine you'll pick it right up."

They arrived at Harris' house, and he turned the horses over to Ruis, and went to check on the small pipes that lay at water's edge At the foot of the hill Harris had fashioned a type of funnel that directed the rising heat from a fireplace to the intake pipes. The heat then transferred from the pipes to the water, taking the chill off the spring water that fed the pool.

Kathleen's mouth dropped open. "You really do have a pool!"

"Yes, and there is a Gazebo there at the side if you care to disrobe. If not, you can take off your shoes and just dangle your feet in the water."

"Are you going to swim?" inquired Kathleen.

"Yes, I love to swim. They had a pool at Notre Dame. Before I went there, I swam in a creek. Pools are nicer as there is no chance of snakes."

Kathleen did not come out of the Gazebo immediately, and

Harris decided she must have elected not to swim. "Kathleen," he said in a teasing tone, "do you need help untying your corset strings?"

"No, I quit wearing a corset at the ranch. There didn't seem to be any point. I am having trouble getting all these stupid buttons undone on my shoes. I hope you have a button hook for later."

"Yes, I do and I'll help you with them later." Harris planned on that being much later, or, at least he hoped so.

Harris disappeared into the Gazebo on the opposite side of the pool and was already in the water when Kathleen emerged from the other Gazebo. She sat on the bench in the Gazebo. and thought about whether she was going to swim or not. She took her time unbuttoning her shoes. She disliked the current shoe fashion. They were so hard to get on and get off, all those pesky buttons.

The last words Fred had spoken to her was that she was going to become a slut. She seemed to be on her way to proving him right. When she exited the Gazebo, it was obvious that she intended to swim. She had decided that since he had seen the bottom half of her body, he might as well see the rest.

As she started down the steps into the pool Harris said, "Stop."

She immediately covered her breasts.

"No don't cover your breasts. I want to see them. They are perfect and beautiful. They look like carved Ivory."

She dived into the pool and quickly swam to the other end. The pool wasn't that long. She turned at the end and floated back to where he was standing in the water. Her breasts were bobbing above the water line.

He leaned over and kissed each of them. She smiled up at him, so he kissed them again. Then he took his arm and placed it under her shoulders and stood her upright. He put his arms around her and kissed her passionately. She could feel his member rising between her legs. She felt a tingle of excitement run through her entire body.

Harris said. "If we're going to do this, let's do it right." He picked her up and carried her out of the pool. Then he wrapped both of them in large Turkish towels. Then he gave her a smaller towel to dry her hair which she had taken down. It was falling around her shoulders like a shawl. Once again he picked her up in his arms, and carried her down the hall to a bedroom.

The first thing Kathleen noticed was how well appointed the room was, thinking, *"His wife obviously had good taste."*

One striking feature was that the bed was from the colonial era. It was high off the floor, and there were three small steps leading up to the bed itself. Kathleen let the towel slip from her when she reached the last step and then pulled back the covers and slipped in between the sheets. They were cool, and she shivered.

Harris joined her and took her into his arms, nuzzled her neck, and said that he would get her warm. They laughed and kissed, then explored each other's body as if they were teenagers just realizing men and women are designed differently. He kissed her as if he couldn't get enough of her. She was eager to accept his mouth and tongue. He then planted kisses all over her face and then started kissing down her neck to her breasts. He caressed and kissed them and sucked on the nipples until they stood as taut pink points.

He felt sure she was ready to receive him, and she definitely was. He glided his member into her and to his delight and surprise, she could take all of him.

Kathleen placed a hand on each of his buttocks and held him in place. She wanted to feel the extent of his member resting inside her. She was overwhelmed with a pleasure she had never felt before. He reveled that his member was completely encased in soft moisture flesh.

Then nature took control and he began the slow in and out thrust. Kathleen sighed with delight. "Oh, yes, Oh, yes" she would murmer. The speed of his movements increased, her back bowed off the bed, and then he emptied himself into her.

He rolled over and took her into his arms, and she was sobbing.

"Did I hurt you?"

"Oh, no, it was wonderful," she sobbed.

"Why are you crying?"

"That's the way I always thought married love should be like."

Her comment distressed Harris. "This woman has been married, and her husband has never given her pleasure in bed. What kind of a beast was he?" Harris continued to kiss and a caress her until she stopped crying.

Just then there was a tap on the bedroom door. Kathleen sat up with a start.

"That's just Ruis. He's left some chilled champagne outside the door," explained Harris.

"You bastard, do you always open a bottle of Champagne after you have bedded a woman?" Kathleen asked angrily.

"Christ, no. He brings me a bottle of Champagne every night, and just knocks on the door and leaves. The Champagne, and your being here have nothing to do with each other. First, you are the only woman who has ever been in this room, much less in this bed."

"You and your wife…?

"NO," said Harris emphatically. "I have had trouble sleeping at night since I got back from Pecos. Ruis places a bottle of champagne outside my door every night, and taps on the door to let me know it is here. Sometimes it just takes a glass or two and some nights nearly the whole bottle before I just pass out and get some sleep."

"Why Champagne?"

"It's my favorite wine. I discovered it when I lived in France. The Brothers don't serve it at the monastery."

"You don't have trouble sleeping there?"

"I did at first," he said, extending a dressing robe to her, and said, "Here slip this on, and join me on the settee by the fireplace."

There were still a few coals burning brightly and giving off a small amount of heat. Even in July in Denver, a small fire in the fireplace is needed.

He put on a gray silvery dressing gown, brought the bottle of champagne into the room and opened it. He opened the beveled doors of a chest high china cabinet which appeared in the fire light to be made of cherry, and brought out two crystal Champagne glasses. Harris filled each glass and handed her one. She was thirsty plus she was embarrassed about her outburst. They were both thirsty after their joint activity, and Harris soon refilled their glasses They had only taken a few sips when Harris' eyes asked the unspoken question, and Kathleen's gave the unspoken "yes".

They were back in bed at once, and he was eagerly using his member. Her legs went stiff and her back bowed, and then he climaxed, and she relaxed back onto the bed. She never wanted him to stop. How wonderful it was for him to fully insert into a woman.

"You had no way of knowing about the bottle of wine. I didn't think to tell you."

"You sleep in here instead of going up stairs?" asked Kathleen.

"Yes, I haven't been upstairs for any reason since Sophie died," he explained.

"I'm sorry, I didn't know that either. I didn't mean to…" apologized Kathleen.

"No, it's all right. You have lost a spouse, too, so you know what it is like."

Kathleen mused to herself, *"Yes, Fred died, but I was relieved not saddened. Maybe I loved him at first, or thought I could."*

He held her in his arms, and she said, "I know what we did was a sin, but it was a wonderful sin."

"No, it was not a sin. God created men and women differently so they could join their bodies together and give each other pleasure. Having to wait until marriage is a man-made rule, probably made by men who had never known the joy of being with a woman. The Lord never said it was a sin."

"You must have gone to a very liberal order of monks."

"Oh, no! They adhere to all the man-made rules of the Church. I believe a man should never force a woman, and

I do agree that if a woman conceives a child, it is the man's responsibility to raise the child, however."

"Conception is not apt to occur in my case, so you needn't worry."

"I wouldn't worry if it were you with child. I would love to raise a child with you."

Kathleen was speechless, and then finally said, "It's late and I need to go home, but I feel so safe and secure with you."

"Why do you want to go home? Have I offended you?"

"Maria will be worried about me," explained Kathleen.

"Is Maria your mother?" asked Harris.

"Of course not, although she has been like a mother to me since I came to the ranch. She already knows I'm a fallen woman."

"All you have done is fall into my arms, and I plan to keep you there forever."

He didn't give her a chance to say anything else, and he announced, "I will go rouse Ruis and get him to go tell Maria you are with me and safe. I'll be right, back."

He wasn't gone five minutes until he returned and found her sound asleep. Her raven black hair was sprayed out over the white pillowcase, and she looked like an angel. He slipped back into bed and propped his head up on his hand and just watched her sleep.

He whispered into the darkness, "Sophie, I am sorry, but I never loved you the way I love this woman."

Kathleen had been a widow for three years; so apparently, her need was a great as his. Then he drifted off to sleep.

As night gave away to day, Kathleen grew restless. Harris

kissed her lightly. Her eyes fluttered open, and it took several seconds before she remembered where she was.

"Good Morning, Kathleen," he whispered.

"How nice it is to be awakened with a good morning kiss."

"Would you like to have a real good morning kiss?" asked Harris.

"If that means what I think it does, I certainly would."

He was in her immediately, and no man could have been more gentle and caring than Harris was that morning. Kathleen responded as a woman in love.

"You didn't cry that time." commented Harris.

"Those were tears of joy and happiness before. Now I am just happy."

"You honor me, Kathleen."

Once again there was a knock on the bedroom door. "Mr. Harris, the breakfast cart is ready."

"Thank you Ruis. I'll get it."

"Mercifully he always knocks," she commented.

"Put the robe back on, darling, and I'll serve you breakfast in bed." She sat up, smoothed the covers, and he placed a silver tray on her lap and lifted the silver dome, and she squealed.

"Eggs Benedict! How did you know I love Eggs Benedict? I haven't had any in a long time."

"I had Ruis ask Marie what you liked for breakfast."

"You are such a dear. Where did you find English Muffins in Denver?" she asked.

"I taught Lewis at the bakery how to make them," he explained.

"You are a man of many talents," she cooed.

"I will be delighted to show you all of them," Harris replied.

Kathleen laughed. "I bet you would!"

Harris sat on the foot of the bed drinking tea and eating scones and watched her eat. He loved even watching her eat. He sat very silently for a long time.

She finished eating, and then he said, "Kathleen, I love you more than I have ever loved anyone. Will you marry me?"

She looked at him bewildered and said, "How can we get married? We don't really know each other except in the Biblical sense!" They had a big laugh over that. "Harris, that is such a compliment, but I can't marry you, yet."

"Yet? What do you mean not yet?' quizzed Harris.

"Well, I just can't. Fred said I was going to end up a slut, and I am afraid that is what I have become."

"You are not a slut, and don't ever say that again!" he said angrily. "You are just a woman who is full of love and caring, and wasn't allowed to show it, apparently. Do know," he said forcefully, "I will do everything that I can, to change the 't' on that word to an 's'. Kathleen, we are already married in the eyes of God, and I truly love you. It's the state of Colorado and the Catholic Church who think they have to give us permission to be happy in our bodily union."

There was a knock on the door. "Again!" Kathleen, said irritated.

"Mr. Harris," said Ruis. "Mr. Harwell is here, and wants to know how soon you can leave to go up to the mine."

Harris said, "Oh, shit. Sorry, Kathleen. Tell Tom I may not go up to the mine today, I'll just work in the office, maybe."

Ruis went outside where Tom Harwell was waiting on horseback. "Mr. Harris said he may not go up to the mine today, he'll just work in the office."

"Work in the office? He hasn't done that in a month." A slight pause later, Tom said, "Oh, is he with someone?"

"It would not be right for me to say. Senor."

Tom laughed loudly and said, "That son of a bitch isn't going anywhere-except maybe to Hell." Tom gave the horse a mild kick with his foot, and rode off, still chuckling.

The atmosphere in the bedroom had become very serious, and Kathleen said, "Harris, before this goes any further, whatever this is, I must tell you about my first marriage."

"No, you don't. I've already figured out a good bit about it. I know it wasn't a happy one for you."

"It's more than that. There are some things you need to know, so you can understand me better. Then you may not want to officially marry me."

"Unless you killed someone, I can't imagine I could ever stop loving you and wanting you to marry me. I want you in my bed every night for the rest of my life."

"I will eagerly agree to be in your bed every night," Harris grabbed her hand and kissed it. She said, "But you must listen to what I have to tell you before I ever agree to marry you."

CHAPTER THREE

The Truth About Fred

"I had known Fred all of my life. I actually can't remember a time when I didn't know him. His father and my father were best friends. I was nine when Fred went off to Christian Brothers University in Memphis. Everyone assumed he would study to become a priest. He was always very devoted to the Catholic faith. Because of the distance, he didn't come home for four years, but he did graduate, with a degree in theological studies. He was traveling back home with a friend. Just for a lark, and to find a place to spend the night, they stopped at the Lazy K ranch."

"Your ranch?" asked Harris.

"Well, yes, the one I own now. It was called the Lazy K Ranch then. Fred and his friend stayed on, and worked for about a year. Fred realized he really liked the work and the idea of being a herdsman. It was so unlike him, it shocked everyone. His father died before he could get home. His father left him a good bit of money, and he decided to buy the ranch and renamed it the Abel Ranch. Once that was settled, he came back to San Francisco to find a bride. He escorted several of us around town. And, always the gentleman, he showed me a wonderful time. After about a month, he asked me to marry him, and I agreed. I was not yet twenty and he seemed so much more mature than the other young men I had been seeing. I suppose that I thought there would be something romantic about being married to a man who owned a ranch."

She continued, "We had a large wedding at the cathedral in San Francisco, and my father hosted a dinner and dance following the ceremony. Everything wound down late afternoon, and then we checked into the Golden Sea Gull Hotel. Our room had a magnificent view of the bay. He handed me a large white leather bound box, and in it was the most beautiful Rosary I had ever seen. The beads were pearls and the ones between them were cut crystal. He said that every night before he goes to bed he says the Rosary, and he wanted us to establish that practice every night, too. Of course I agreed, he was now my husband. After we said the complete Rosary, I excused myself to get ready for bed, and I changed into a lovely gown and robe my cousin had given me. It was modest, I was well covered. It was decorated with lace and embroidered flowers. He frowned when he saw me."

Harris listened intently, "He turned off the lamp and told me to take off the gown. I did, and got into bed with him. He rolled over on me and rammed himself into me."

"Wait a minute. No foreplay, no hugging or kissing or anything?" Harris said in disbelief.

"No, he just plowed into me. It hurt so bad I screamed. He clamped his hand over my mouth and told me to be quiet. He finished quickly, thank goodness, and then kissed me fully on the mouth for the first and last time."

Harris just gaped at her. "How could he…you mean he never kissed you again?"

"No, and not like that. He said his being in me would hurt less, as I got used to it. He was overjoyed to find I was a virgin. I don't know why he thought I wouldn't be. I didn't know being a virgin was that important to a man. I didn't realize every girl wasn't a virgin. Except in the case of my cousin, Tommy. He bedded several girls, until he found one who enjoyed it as much as he did. He married her immediately. They have now been married six years and have four children and one on the way. Usually girls and boys don't talk about such things, but Tommy and I were close. We were quite fond of each other and would have married, but we were cousins. Tommy explained the male anatomy to me and how they each functioned,"

"So you and Tommy never…?" asked Harris

"Oh, no," said Kathleen.

"You are sweet and innocent, Kathleen. Many girls aren't virgins but pretend to be."

"How is that possible?" she asked.

"I'll explain it sometime," said Harris.

"I certainly don't need to know it now," she laughed. "Fred said he wouldn't touch me again until I had stopped bleeding from my broken hymen. I didn't realize there would be so much blood."

Kathleen continued after a pause, "One of Fred's friends had loaned us a 30 foot sailboat and completely stocked it with non-perishable food, smoked meat, and other goodies and a lot of wine. Really, there was a lot of wine and whiskey. The yacht had a small galley and a bedroom that slept two."

Kathleen calmed a little as she continued, "The next several days, we sailed around the bay and Fred taught me how to crew. We had a good time doing that. On the fourth day we set out to open sea. We always stayed within sight of land, and anchored at night in some cove. It took us three of four days to get down the coast, and at twilight on the last day we sailed into Monterey Bay. We docked at the wharf and then climbed the stairs up to walk where all the wonderful sea food cafes were, and ate the fresh catch of the day."

She continued, "After we said the Rosary, I had to tell him the bleeding had stopped. He extinguished all the lamps and candles and told me not to bother with a night gown, just to get in bed and spread my legs."

Harris looked appalled as she continued. "Fred forced himself into me and it hurt nearly as bad as the first night. He kissed me on the cheek and said, thank you. The evening before, he had spotted a Catholic Church on the hill above the wharf. It turned out to be one of Father Sierra's original missions. We went to early Mass, and then had breakfast."

"What did you do during the day?" asked Harris.

"We sailed around the bay some, Fred would fish; I would read, or just dose in the sun. I did some needlework. That is how most days went. We slept a little late one morning and didn't make it to six o'clock Mass, but there was also one at seven. The gift store, that was attached to the church was open then, and we went in. Fred bought five plain gray nightgowns, that I assumed were made for nuns. He didn't ask if I wanted them, or not, and

I had plenty of night gowns. I thought maybe he was going to give them to some convent."

"That night I drank a very large amount of wine, as I knew what was about to happen. Maybe it was the wine, maybe I was just getting used to it, but my body started responding to his. He stopped in mid thrust and told me to stop it. He said that he forgave me, because my mother had died young, and I had no one to instruct me on how Catholic women should act in bed."

Harris just shook his head.

"That wasn't quite true, because my father had arranged for my cousin, who had been married about six months, to talk to me. What she described, and what I expected, was nothing like what I was receiving from Fred. One night I offered him my breasts, and he got furious. He said that the only purpose for breasts was to feed children, and I appeared to be more than capable of that. Any other use would cause the husband to lust. And lust was a sin. I had no idea what lust was. If it were a sin, I did not want to be involved."

"How did you feel about all of that?" Harris asked.

"I was crushed. It was as if I were a naughty school girl being lectured by a head master. I cried, and he told me I should cry, because of the way I acted."

"That's why you were so still the first time I made love to you," remarked Harris.

"Yes, but I like it better your way."

"I'm glad. A woman should get as much pleasure from love making as the man."

"I don't know if Fred got any pleasure or not. He may have considered pleasure a sin. The evening before we headed back, Fred gathered up all the nightgowns that my friends and family had given me. They were so lovely. He put them into a burlap bag and added a large rock, that he had retrieved from the shore, and threw the full bag overboard. I screamed, 'Those gowns were mine, and you had no right to throw them into the bay.'"

Fred said, "Everything you own is mine. They are the work of the devil and will tempt me to lust after you."

"Again, I heard that lust is a sin. I cried myself to sleep that night in a desk chair. At least I didn't have to endure him that night. I don't think the nuns ever talked to us about lust. It must have been so bad they couldn't talk to us about it."

Harris took her face in his hands and said, "You are such a dear, sweet person."

"When we got back to San Francisco, there was a round of parties. I smiled and acted the part of the happy bride. My cousin, who had talked to me about marriage, had moved to Seattle, so I had no one to talk to about the situation. I was married to Fred, and that was it."

Harris seethed in silence as she continued. "We finally got to the ranch, and that is when I first met Maria. I was awed by the size of the ranch and the operation of it. The ranch house was originally just a one storey adobe, but Fred had added a second floor over the downstairs bedroom. There was an alcove to the side of the upstairs bedroom which was where he kept the records for the ranch. Then there is a door that leads to a small landing and a flight of stairs that leads to a ground floor patio. The patio was walled in for privacy."

She paused, then continued, "The nightly ritual continued without change. After about six weeks I started my womanly flow. I knew that most of my friends had a flow every month, but I didn't. I only had a flow several times a year. Fred was sure

I was with child and was so thrilled. I tried to tell him I wasn't with child. He would have it no other way. So he put me to bed until the flow stopped. Since I was cramping he was sure I had miscarried. This happened three more times that year and each time he was sure I had miscarried."

Harris touched her hand gently as she continued, "After the third time, Fred insisted we go to town and see Dr. Murphy. He examined both of us, and told us that my womb was titled in such a way, that it would be impossible for me to conceive a child. Fred was furious. He all but dragged me out of the office, down the stairs and into the buggy. He drove like a madman, and didn't stop to water the horses. It was almost dark by the time we got home. He handed the horses off to the stable boys, and stormed into house ahead of me. As soon as I got inside, and closed the door, he hit me in the face with his fist. I fell to the floor and screamed."

I asked, "Why did you do that?"

"Why didn't you tell me you couldn't have children?"

"How would I know?"

"Didn't you see a doctor before we married?"

"No, I didn't know anything was wrong."

He took off his belt, yanked my skirts up to my waist and started whipping me on my legs with the belt, and kicking me in the ribs and stomach."

"The son-of-a-bitch! If I had known, I would have killed him," Harris declared.

"I screamed and screamed and begged him to stop, but the more I screamed the harder he hit. I stopped screaming hoping he would quit. Finally I said, I was a virgin when we married, how could I have known."

Harris wanted to say something but she wouldn't let him and continued. "Either that made sense to him, or his arm was tired. He walked away, and I fainted. I don't know how much time passed before I came to. It was pitch black and I could hear Fred snoring upstairs."

"I tried to get up and could not. I started crawling through the great room thinking that if I could make it through the parlor, and into the bedroom, maybe I could lift myself up onto the bed. I got as far as the middle of the parlor floor and passed out again."

"That's where Fred found me the next morning, and ordered me to get up. When he saw I couldn't, he yanked me up and dragged me into the bedroom, and sat me down on the chamber pot chair. He showed a little concern that I had passed some blood, but said that would clear up after a couple of weeks in bed. He helped me into the bed. I asked if I could have some coffee. He said he didn't have time to fool with it as he and Carlos and some of the men, were going to the far end of the spread. They believed the wolves were getting in and eating the sheep. He did pour me a glass of water from the pitcher on the vanity table."

Harris pounded his fists together as she spoke, "He gave me a stern warning that I wasn't to get out of bed, and I was not to go outside until all the bruises were gone. As if I were in any condition to go anywhere. Again, I asked for coffee. He once again said he didn't have time to fool with it. Fred said he and the men would not be back until late afternoon."

Harris was beside himself with anger. "Fred didn't even tell you he was sorry?"

"No, and what hurt me worse than what he said, "When I

think of all the sperm I wasted on you. Then he stomped out of the room. I realized then he had married me for breeding purposes only, because he knew my blood line."

Kathleen collapsed onto Harris' chest and cried angry, bitter tears. He stroked her hair and let her cry as long as she needed to. The hurt and anger she had held inside her for three years finally came out.

"Kathleen, I love you and will always protect you and keep you safe. I will not pressure you into marrying me, but I am going to marry you right now."

"What do you mean?"

"Kathleen O'Brien King, I promise to love you, cherish you, be faithful to you totally, in sickness and in health and honor you every way that I can for as long as I live. With my worldly goods I thee endow. And I will protect you forever."

He smiled and said, "Those are the same promises I would make before a priest, and I just made them to God. I meant every word of what I just said. I consider myself spiritually married to you, whether you ever agree to go before a priest and make the same promises. I am yours."

She started crying again. "I didn't mean to make you cry, please stop crying, and give me a smile." She smiled, and he kissed her tenderly.

"I don't want to upset you, but what happened after the bruises cleared up?"

"Fred finally said that I could sit on the front porch in the rocker, but I was to never come upstairs again, unless invited. He moved my clothes to the armoire in the downstairs bedroom. About two months afterwards, one night he said, 'I need you upstairs tonight, but you are not to spend the night.' He had already said the Rosary, so other than that it was the same as it ever was. My invitation, or command, to come upstairs. happened every two months or so. It was always the same ordeal."

"About an hour after he left that morning, Maria slipped into the house. She had made sure the men hadn't doubled back. When she saw me she gasped, and that confirmed what I believed my face looked like. My left eye was swollen shut."

"Good Lord," exclaimed Harris.

"Maria then brought me a bowl of broth, and a mug of coffee. I told her that Fred must never know she had been there."

"I know Miss Kathleen. All the women could hear your screams, and they knew he was beating you, but there was nothing we could do. He would have shot us. All the women came to my place, and we prayed to the Holy Virgin for him to stop beating you."

"How did you know he was beating me?"

"A woman screams differently in childbirth, or if she is frightened, or is delighted about something, but the screams of a woman being beaten are entirely different from those."

"That night Fred brought me a supper tray, and one of the ugly night gowns. There was no evidence Maria had been there, as I would not let her clean up the blood on my legs. Fred handed me a wet cloth and said for me to do it."

"What a bastard!" hissed Harris. "After you healed, how did you spend your time?"

"I helped in the vegetable garden with the other women. We grow a lot of our own food and put up as much of it as we can for the winter. We have a flock of chickens and several milk cows so we only have to buy things like flour, coffee and things like that to see us through the winter."

"No pigs or hogs?"

"Never! Fred said the Bible was quite clear that people should not eat the meat of an animal with a split hoof."

"I've seen you eat ham."

"That was Fred's rule, not mine. I wished he had paid more attention to other parts of the Bible, like what it says about love. I planted a lot of flowers which became my pet project, but I had to be careful about how much water I used which was strange, because we have three streams that run all spring and summer from melting snow in the mountains."

"He just wanted to remind you he had control." said Harris.

"I didn't need to be reminded. I had a small loom and an endless supply of wool thread. I would card the wool and then spin it into thread. We already had a spinning wheel. I asked if I could have a large loom with foot pedals on it. He agreed and I made everyone on the ranch new ponchos, bed blankets, wool vests, and just about anything that could be made from wool. Fred seemed to be pleased about that although he never came right out and praised me."

"Unbelievable," commented Harris.

"Finally, when I had nearly run out of things to make, since wool garments last a long time, I experimented with some new types of dye and made what became wall hangings. The Mexican family thought they were beautiful. Fred took several of them into town to Marauder's Hardware Store. Carlos came back from town one day, and said they were displayed in the front window of the store."

"Wait a minute. I think I have one of those. It's in various shades of purple and it looks like the mountains."

"That sounds like one I made."

"I have it upstairs," said Harris. "I just love it. I had no idea you made it. I'll have Ruis go upstairs tomorrow and bring it down."

"You still don't go upstairs?" asked Kathleen.

"No, there are too many bad memories, but after we are officially married, I want you to redecorate that room from the wall paper out. Even remove the fireplace mantle. Then it will be just our special place."

"I love the room we use now," said Kathleen.

"I love it because you are in it with me, but I want to banish all the old memories, and make full use of the house."

"Fred believed that the light of a full moon increased fertility. We tried that every full moon all one summer to no avail. We had an extra mattress which he put on the floor of the down stair patio, so we could do the act in the light of the full moon."

"There was one rule I had to obey. I had to keep my eyes closed at all times. I assumed he kept his eyes closed too. One night I don't know what came over me, but I opened an eye and saw that he had a full erection. I promptly mounted him and gave him the ride of his life. He was shouting for me to get off, but we both knew any quick movement with him, in that state, could cause damage. When it was over, I rolled into a tight ball expecting the beating to start the next minute. He started up the stairs, and screamed at me that I was going to become nothing but a slut. And he said that I was on my way to spreading my legs for any man who asked. He said he noticed how the men on the ranch looked at me."

I said, "Yes, but I never look back."

"Give you time and you will," he retorted and he walked into the bedroom. He was headed for his belt I was sure. But nothing happened. The next morning I woke up still rolled in a ball, but freezing to death. I grabbed the quilt on the mattress, pulled it up around me and went upstairs to face whatever punishment he had in store for me. He wasn't in the bedroom so I went downstairs and looked out the front window. I saw him in his best black suit, black boots and new black hat about to mount his horse. I assumed he was going into town to change the will, get a divorce or an annulment. Whatever was going to happen didn't mean good news for me."

"He had ridden about halfway to the main gate when he slumped in the saddle and then started sliding off the horse. The stable boys were standing nearby, and they ran to him. I dashed out to him still wrapped in a quilt. He was on the ground and was dead. There was absolutely no pulse."

"Carlos had one of the young men run to the Spanish Mission and get the priest. The priest came and gave Fred the last rites, but it was too late. Several of the men picked Fred's body up and placed him on the dining table in the great room. They folded his hands, and I placed the Rosary, he had given me as a wedding present. in his hands. As is the Mexican custom they placed candles on tall wooden candle holders at the four corners of the table where they had placed Fred's body."

"Three men sat up all night with his corpse. The funeral mass was the next day at the mission. The ranch carpenter made a coffin and we lined it with a silk blanket Maria acquired from someplace. She got me a black hat with a black veil, to hide the face of the grieving widow. I imagine she knew I wasn't grieving, but nervous and scared about what would happen to me."

"Carlos and six of the men took the coffin into the high pastures and buried him. Carlos said they put a lot of rocks on the top of his grave and one long flat stone. They were gone overnight so it must be quite a distance."

"You didn't go with them?"

"No, and I don't know where the grave is either."

"Did you bury him with your Rosary?" asked Harris.

"Yes, I had come to hate it and wanted nothing to remind me of him. I haven't said the Rosary since his death. Now, are you sure you want to marry me?" Kathleen asked.

"Remember, I have already married you. You have to decide if you want to marry me."

"Well, there's more," Kathleen continued. "I didn't go to town for about three months, so no one in town knew he was dead. Then I put a notice in the paper about his death. I waited so that I could get things settled, before one of his cousins could get word of his death and try to break the will."

"It stated that the children and I were to inherit the ranch, and I was to live there the rest of my natural life if I so desired. Obviously the will was written before our marriage. The lawyer said that although there were no children, Fred had intended for me to live on the ranch the rest of my life. No cousins ever appeared however. Not many city folks want to raise sheep."

"I am sorry you had to go through all that. Love is a mighty healer, and I would like to be the one to heal you, if you will let me," Harris said softly.

"Only if you don't insist that I marry you, just yet," stated Kathleen.

"I'm married to you and very happy; whenever you are ready to make it official, I promise you, I will make you very happy," restated Harris. "Look at the time. I had no idea it was early afternoon," he exclaimed. "Let's go over to the Frontier Grill. I'm hungry for a T-bone steak." He was thinking, *"I'm going to need a lot of strength, as I plan to do a lot of healing tonight."* Harris simply could not get enough of her body.

"That sounds good," Kathleen said. "I am so wrung out from reliving all that, I need something to build my strength back up."

CHAPTER FOUR

Life after Fred

They entered the Frontier Grill and were greeted by Josh Logan, the owner. The waiter brought them glasses of water and menus. It didn't take long for them to order steaks.

"How do you like you steak, Kathleen?" he asked.

"Medium rare, please."

"Make mine the same way," added Harris. The steaks arrived quickly with cottage fried potatoes and thick slices of tomatoes.

Kathleen said, "I told you about my first marriage, now it is your turn."

"No, not yet," replied Harris.

"Not yet?" questioned Kathleen.

"Isn't 'yet' your favorite word?" chuckled Harris. "I will tell you about my life starting at the beginning, although the first part of it will be what others have told me. Tom said my father was killed at the Battle of Van Buren, Arkansas, and my mother died having me."

"Oh, I am so sorry."

Harris went on to explain, "I have always been well taken

care of. I was told that my mother died while at her great grandmother's house in Barling, Arkansas. A few years later my great grandmother died, I'm not sure what her name was. I was then placed in a Catholic orphanage run by the Benedictine Sisters at Shoal Creek, Arkansas. They had built a large convent there. The convent consisted of four, three story buildings placed to form a large rectangle. All the orphans, of all ages, were housed on the third floor which was divided into two sections."

"What were your parents names?" she asked.

"My father was John McGinty, and my mother's last name was Harris. But I was always called Harris McGinty. My father fought for the Union, but apparently people in Arkansas didn't care for the Yankees, as they called them."

"Harris McGinty is a very distinctive name," commented Kathleen.

"All of the orphans were well taken care of by the sisters, and I loved them very much. The yard in the middle of the convent was where the older children would play, or the sisters would take the babies out to get some sunshine in nice weather. They also ran a school in connection with the convent, so I attended grammar school there, too. When I was about nine years old, Sister Mary Joseph and Mary Ignatius took me into Bonneville, the closest town to buy me some new shoes. I had outgrown the ones I was wearing. There were several town ladies coming out of the store. That was the first time I had seen a woman who did not have on a habit, and it scared me to death. I got behind Sister Mary Joseph's habit and hid in the folds."

She said, "Child, what on earth is the matter with you?"

"What did those women do to be excommunicated?"

"They both really laughed, and said, Harris, that is how

women dress who decided to get married and have children. They have done nothing wrong. We wear these habits because we are Brides of Christ."

"Will Jesus ever give you children?"

"Why yes, we have several hundred children. You are one of them that the Lord has entrusted to our care, because your parents have gone on to Heaven."

"How sweet of them to put it that way!" Kathleen said. "Bless your heart."

"I know that sounds dumb, but I had never seen a woman that didn't have on the black and white habit. When it came time for me to go to high school, I was sent to St. Scholastica Convent in Fort Smith, Arkansas. The same order of sisters ran the high school for boys, and a separate one for girls."

"Did they ever let the boys and the girls have parties together?" asked Kathleen.

"About once a month, if that much, we would have dances. The girls wore white gloves, and the sisters kept an eagle eye out. They insisted that we dance far enough apart that our guardian angels could be between us. All of us dreaded dance night. The boys had to wear a suit, tie and an over-starched shirt."

"The boys' teachers were mostly monks or priests, and they would play ball with the boys when the weather was warm, and in the summer they would take us fishing."

"Where did you go to college?"

"The administrators of my trust fund insisted that I go to Notre Dame to be trained by the Jesuits. After daily Mass, we would have theological instruction and questions."

"Questions?"

"Yes, the Jesuits were keen on training a man's mind. The

priests would also give us very stern lessons on how it was a sin to look at a girl with unhealthy thoughts in our minds, and scared us to death to even think about a girl at all."

"A lesson you took to heart!" teased Kathleen.

Harris laughed, "Well, at that time, at least."

Harris continued, "It wasn't until one of my classmates remarked he wouldn't be coming back to school the next year because his father had lost his job and couldn't afford the tuition and uniforms. I was completely puzzled. I went to the Mother Superior's office and told her of my confusion."

"It was then that I learned that all of my clothing, schooling and everything else, had been paid for by a trust, that an unnamed person had set up for me."

"But, who? I asked her."

"All I knew then was Mother Superior said the law firm of Bowen and Dorsey in Fort Smith handled all of the money. They never would tell me, so I don't know who my kind benefactor was back then. I discovered who it was years later."

Kathleen listened sympathetically as he continued, "I was stunned. I guess I thought Jesus just provided everything. It troubled me a great deal. That is when it finally really soaked in that I was an orphan. I just was never the 'poor little orphan boy.' However, I asked Mother Superior if the trust would pay for my friend Mike's schooling. She said it wasn't possible. The money had been set aside for my use only. I really struggled with that."

"Then, I started worrying about whether or not the money would run out. Mother Superior told me it was a sin to worry about money. I concentrated on my studies and graduated from high school with the top marks in the class."

"That doesn't surprise me," said Kathleen as she gave him a

light kiss on the check. They were in a booth so she was sure no one could see her do that.

"Mother Superior called me in about a month before graduation and said that my trustee insisted I to go to Notre Dame to study with the Jesuits. She didn't seem too pleased it was going to be the Jesuits, but it wasn't her choice. The trustee wanted me to major in engineering and or accounting. He, I guessed it was a he, anyway, heard I was very good with numbers. I had never given any thought of going to college, but I was thrilled beyond my wildest dreams. I would have majored in music and art if that is what the mysterious 'he' had wanted."

Kathleen settled back and listened as he continued, "I was really sad to leave the sisters, and the priests. They had been my parents all my life. Before I left, one of the older priests sat me down and gave me a very detailed description of how babies are made. I had heard whispers on the playground, but Father Smith wiped away all doubts. He said that if a baby was conceived outside of marriage, in a Catholic Church, the parents would burn in Hell for eternity. That scared the hell out of me, literally. He also mentioned self-abuse but was not specific about it. That I discovered on my own."

Kathleen gave him a slight grin. "I went first by stage coach and then by railroad to South Bend, Indiana. I lived in a dormitory which was no adjustment for me, but some of the boys apparently were homesick. I thought it was a wonderful adventure. I wondered why I wasn't asked to study to be a priest, as many of the young men were there for that specific purpose. I found out much later that my benefactor was not a practicing Catholic, which troubled me even more. That meant he was going to Hell, or that's what I thought at the time, but he was paying for everything in my life. I hoped God would look the other way when he died."

Peach cobbler arrived. They hadn't remembered ordering it but it was too delicious to send back. Harris said, "We either need to eat this fast, or take it home."

"Home, if you mean your house, is fine with me. Have them pack it up to take with us."

Harris said, "Home is our house, because I have married you so it belongs to us now. Just as it is our bed."

Harris helped her into the buggy and she kissed him lightly on the lips. He asked, "Do you want to go for a swim?"

"Not until our food has settled."

"Think you will be too full for dessert or anything else?"

"I'm sure I could be tempted, if the right man asked me."

"I am sure I am the right man."

"I'm sure, too."

On the way home Kathleen asked, "What happened after you went to Notre Dame?"

"Believe it or not I really liked it. I had received a good education, but the Jesuits really challenged my mind. I guess that is why I was sent there."

"What did you do during the summer"?

"Stayed at the Jesuit monastery there. Ten of us lived too far away to go home and I didn't really have a home to go back to."

"What about holidays?"

"At Thanksgiving and Christmas we were farmed out to Catholic families in the area. I was always treated very kindly. I guess I felt more like an orphan at that time than any other. I was used to living with a lot of people around, but I saw how the parents loved their children, and the children loved them back."

Kathleen sensed the pain in this statement. "We were allowed to court the young Catholic girls in town. They would invite us to dances and parties. That final year I did introduce several of the young girls into womanhood."

"You wicked person," she said with a grin. "It's a wonder you didn't get kicked out of school."

"I only confessed it once. By then I had decided a lot of the rules of the church were man made rules probably formulated by virginal old men. If God hadn't intended men and women to join their bodies, He should have made them differently. Two boys did get kicked out for committing some terrible sin but nobody would tell why. It was all very secret."

He continued, "The spring of my senior year an ad appeared in the South Bend newspaper and Father Jerome showed it to me. It was a job opening for a new graduate of Notre Dame with a degree in either engineering or accounting who would be interested in working in the mining industry in Colorado and liked to travel. I answered the ad immediately as I had no idea what I would do after I graduated. The ad was for employment with the Harwell Mines in Denver."

"You can't be serious," exclaimed Kathleen.

"Yes, but I had no idea who Thomas Harwell was or anything about the Harwell mines at that time. I wrote Tom and had several of my teachers write on my behalf. We exchanged several letters and then several telegrams, and he hired me sight unseen. Well, I did send him a photograph. He hired me and then asked me instead of coming straight to Denver, to go to Europe."

"Europe?"

"Yes, I toured the mines in England, Belgium and France, and took notes and then brought a report of all my findings to

Denver. He wanted to know all about the mines in Europe, how much they paid their employees, what the safety precautions were, and there were many."

"That's like a fairy tale."

"I know, and he sent me salary money plus travel money. I was overwhelmed. I didn't know there was that much money in the world. I did have to get permission from my trust to take the job and go but they readily agreed to it."

"Then it was while you were in England you learned about English muffins and scones."

"Yes, and I also went to the mines in Wales."

"What did you learn in France?" asked Kathleen.

"How to properly make love to a woman," he responded.

"Do they have classes?" teased Kathleen.

"Only very private ones. Everybody does it with whomever they please in France."

"Just knowing that, would have put Fred in the grave," pointed out Kathleen.

"It was in France that I found the only other woman who could accommodate all of my member. She was a good teacher too. I learned a lot of things about pleasure from her."

"I think I'll ask a blessing for her" teased Kathleen, "Or send her a thank you note."

"Why?" asked Harris. "She was a whore who earned her living that way."

"I have her to thank for the way you treat me in the bed," she explained.

"You flatter me, Madam."

"Maybe I haven't learned as much as I could," she said smiling impishly.

"Well, it is high time then for another lesson," he agreed.

The packed up food was quickly put away because she was more than ready to receive him. She elevated her hips, wrapped her legs around the small of his back. and was an active participant in the sex act. After the lesson was completed, both were gasping for air and Kathleen could barely talk.

"I hope (gasp), that was (gasp) the final (gasp) lesson."

"Why?" Harris asked incredulously.

"If you give me any more pleasure than what you just did, I think I would have a heart attack."

After Kathleen recovered she returned the discussion to his past. "Then after you finished your inspections in Europe you came to Denver."

"Yes. I sailed from Southhampton to New York City, then made my way to the Transnational Railroad, and then by stagecoach to Denver. I had wired Tom I was back in this country and when to expect me. He said for me to spend the night at the New Frontier Hotel and take my meals there. He owns the hotel."

He continued, "I arrived at their house at the appointment time. For whatever reason, Tom hadn't told Maggie I was coming. When I rang the doorbell, Maggie opened the door and promptly fainted. I called for help and Tom and Bernard, his house man, and Bernard's wife came running. We got her to a liaise in the sun room and she came-to fairly quickly. I thought she was with child, and somehow I had frightened her. Tom just said she hadn't been feeling well, and not to trouble myself, if I startled her. So, that brings us up to now."

"She saw this handsome young man with a mop of curly black hair, and she was just overcome," Kathleen teased.

CHAPTER FIVE

Life continues

After her good morning kiss from Harris, and breakfast again served in bed, Kathleen went to town to meet Carlos and Marie to buy supplies for the ranch. They needed to lay in supplies for the fall and winter, and she wanted to get the freshest supplies before the rush began. Kathleen had offered to cook supper for Harris at her house, and pointed out that since Marie would be going back to the ranch, they would have the house to themselves.

He kissed her on the neck and said, "I really have to go up to the mines with Tom. We won't be back until early dark, but I will look forward to having supper prepared by you."

"I am not a very good cook. Marie and the women at the ranch do all the cooking for the community."

"That's all right. I am mostly interested in dessert," said Harris. He gave her a light pat on her rear and left.

Marie and Carlos were waiting for her when she got to the supply store. They brought two flatbed wagons. Kathleen would fill them before they started back to the ranch. She purchased two, hundred pound bags of coffee beans; four hundred pounds of flour. She made sure the pattern on the flour sacks matched, as the women liked to use the empty flour sacks to make clothes for their children; and then four sacks of corn meal. Kathleen's next big project for the ranch was to put in its own mill. *"Maybe next spring,"* she thought. She had seen a new fandangled machine in a magazine that sewed clothes. She stood and looked at the gadget and decided to get one. Mr. Marauder promised her it worked.

She then bought four bolts of cloth. All women liked new clothes and sewing clothes on that machine will keep the women occupied all winter. They would have to continue making their own patterns for clothes. The printed patterns were written in English.

She then added two large buckets of lard, since they didn't have hogs to render the fat. There was always soap, lots of soap. Most farmers and ranchers made their own using fireplace ashes and lye, but again no lard from pigs. She did not miss the smell that a pig pen would cause. That is why Fred had placed the sheep pens well beyond the living area. Unless the wind shifted, and it usually blew straight west to east, there was no problem. Kathleen had Carlos pick out what ranching supplies they would need to take care of the sheep when they came down from the high pastures.

Maria noticed how happy Miss Kathleen looked, but said nothing. She had a good idea as to why. She and Carlos left for the ranch, loaded down with supplies. Kathleen went back to her house and poured over several recipe books trying to find something she could prepare.

Marie had given her some cooking lessons, but Fred had discouraged her from learning. "Let the Mexicans do it," he said.

CHAPTER SIX

The Elephant On the Trail

Tom and Harris started on the long winding path that would bring them back down the mountain to town. They talked for a while about the mines, the miners and everything except the question playing on Tom's mind.

Tom cleared his throat and said, "How are things going with you and the Widow King?"

"Just fine. Please stop calling her the Widow King," pleaded Harris. "Her name is Kathleen."

"Is this your last fling before going back to Pecos?" inquired Tom.

"No, I am not going back to the Monastery."

"Did you decide city life was more to your liking, or is it that Kathleen has changed you mind?"

"I am in love with Kathleen and have asked her to marry me."

"Great Scott, you work fast. When is the wedding date?" asked Tom.

"There isn't one. She turned me down."

"You are pulling my leg. No woman in her right mind would refuse to marry a handsome, rich man. I ask this only because you are family. Has she enjoyed the pleasure of your magic wand?"

"Gentlemen don't like to kiss and tell, but since you are family 'Yes', she has. She said she couldn't marry me, yet."

"Yet? What's she waiting for? Does she know you are rich?"

"NO," replied Harris. "I guess she loves the ranch more than she loves me."

"Then marry someone else," Tom urged. "There are a number of women who would likely marry you. We need to get that thing of yours off the street, or no woman in Denver is going to be safe."

"The ones over sixty would probably be safe enough," Harris said with a tinge of bitterness mixed with humor.

"I don't want to marry, or be with anyone, but Kathleen. If she doesn't agree to marry me in a reasonable length of time, I will go back to the Monastery. If I am going to be celibate, then it might as well be around other celibate men. I wasn't unhappy there. It was like returning to the womb."

The middle of the afternoon, Ruis knocked on the door and delivered an envelope to Kathleen. He waited while she opened it. A slight look of disappointment, and some relief, registered on her face. She didn't have to cook supper. The Harwell's had invited them to dinner at their mansion. She had heard what a grand place it was, and was eager to see it.

Kathleen wore her best navy blue suit with the extra wide

lapels that lapped over to form a V shape, and a skirt over multiple petticoats. She had a beautiful hat with a peacock feather on it, but she knew a hat would be inappropriate for dining at home. The Harwells had already seen her, but only in evening clothes. She still wanted to make a good impression.

When they arrived at the house, which was about two miles out of town, Kathleen was impressed with its size. The gates of the estate were wide open and gave a sweeping view of the whole estate and the mansion. It was all impressive, especially with snow-capped mountains in the background.

Ruis helped her down from the carriage, walked her to the front door and opened it for her. When Maggie saw her, she out stretched her arms and said, "I am so glad to see you."

Tom boomed from the dining room, "Welcome to the family." Kathleen felt the heat rise to her face. Tom continued, "Anyone who is a friend of Harris is a member of our family. Come right on in." That startled Kathleen, plus she blushed. Maggie stretched out her arms and reiterated Tom's welcome.

The furnishings of the large living room were of the highest quality workmanship and well arranged. Elegant but comfortable was the atmosphere.

About that time Harris came down the stairs with a blonde-haired cherub in his arms. "Kathleen, I would like you to meet my daughter, Annie. She is a year old."

"I did not know you had a daughter," stated Kathleen.

"Forgive me if I did not tell you. I didn't mean to conceal it," apologized Harris.

If Harris told her he had a daughter, she hadn't remembered it. She knew he had been married.

"No problem. I am just surprised. She must have got the blonde hair from her mother," observed Kathleen.

"Yes, and her delicate features from her, too," Maggie added as she stepped into the living room, realizing what a delicate topic they were skirting. "I'll take her upstairs to join Tommy. They adore each other. He is just a month older than Annie." A nanny appeared and reclaimed the baby. Harris kissed Annie on the check before for handing her over.

"Come, let's eat. Mildred has fixed her famous venison roast," said Maggie.

"*Fixed it?* What had been wrong with it?" It would be rude to ask, but Kathleen's interest in eating venison diminished.

Harris noticed the mildly puzzled look on her face. He guessed what was going on in her mind. "Kathleen, in the South, people use the word 'fix' to mean prepare. It's not uncommon to hear someone say, I'm fixing to go to town. Mildred has prepared the venison. There was nothing wrong with it."

Kathleen was thoroughly embarrassed. "I wish you weren't a mind reader," she confessed.

Maggie laughed. "Don't be embarrassed. We southerners often use expressions that other people find peculiar. I have been careful not to ask you if I could 'carry' you someplace. That's another southern expression."

Trying to change the subject, Kathleen asked Maggie where she was from.

"Oh, a little town in Georgia. I'm sure you have never heard of it. It's Ringgold, almost on the Tennessee line."

Finally dinner was over, and Tom and Harris retired to Tom's office room for the usual cigars and brandy. That's the only room in the house where Maggie would let him smoke, as long as he opened the French door onto the terrace. Maggie asked Kathleen if she would like to help put the babies to bed. Kathleen was delighted to be asked, although she knew virtually nothing about children, as she was an only child. Maggie explained that she wanted to be the one the babies saw the last thing at night.

"The nanny takes care of them most of the time. But I like to be the one to tuck them in at night. When they are older I will read them a bedtime story." Maggie finished changing their diapers, and then the ladies joined the men downstairs.

Kathleen tried to stifle a yawn, but Harris saw it, and said, "This dear lady is tired. I think it best if I take her home."

"Finally!" thought Kathleen. They bid their good-nights, and Ruis had the carriage waiting for them before the front door.

"Is Ruis going to walk home?" Kathleen asked.

"No, he has a girlfriend in town, and he will spend the night with her."

"Are they going to be married?"

"Ruis said he wouldn't marry his girlfriend until you married me."

There was a grove of trees before one got to the front gate and the view from the house was blocked. Harris pulled the carriage over, then put his arms around Kathleen and kissed her passionately. She returned his kisses eagerly and started unbuttoning her suit coat and blouse so Harris could get to her breasts.

Breathless, Harris said," Kathleen, I know how to have sex in a carriage, but I don't want to just have sex, I want to make love to you."

"How fast can the horses go?" she asked.

Harris popped the reins and the horses started off at a good clip.

The door had hardly been shut, and Tom swatted Maggie on her behind. "Still from Georgia, huh? Where did you ever hear of that town?"

"I'm not sure. I may have made it up. I am not about to tell Harris I'm from Arkansas. That could bring on too many questions I don't want to answer. I'd rather lie about where I am from than to lie about not knowing his mother and father."

"Damn John McGinty for committing suicide anyways," said Tom.

"Are your ever going to tell Harris the truth?"

"When I die the lawyer will give him a notarized letter telling him I was the source of the Trust. I don't think his life will be any better if he knows his parents never married, and his mother was a Confederate spy whore. John had asked Carolyn to marry him," Tom informed Maggie. "That was before we realized she betrayed us and nearly got me killed."

"Telling him I am from Georgia, is no worse than to make him think you are just from Kansas, and his father died in the Battle of Van Buren."

"I suppose not."

"Harris and Kathleen seem so happy together," Maggie said.

"Yes, he has asked her to marry him, but she refused."

"She refused? I can't believe it." exclaimed Maggie. "She has been married so she couldn't be a virgin, if that's the problem."

"You know Harris has never had a problem with seducing

women, so she does have knowledge of all his talents. He said she loves the ranch more than she loves him."

"I am so sorry, that really depresses me. That means he is going back to Pecos," lamented Maggie.

"I'm not sure; he thinks he can get her to change her mind."

"Let's go to bed, General Harwell. I am very weary."

Kathleen went on into the house ahead of Harris while he fed and bedded down the horses for the night. Harris had discarded most of his clothes as he ran down the hall to the bedroom. She was in bed, naked and waiting for him and was ready to receive him. He plunged into her and his movements were hard and fast.

He finished quickly and rolled over and said, "I am so sorry."

"Sorry about what?"

"That I was so rough, but I just couldn't wait to be in you."

"If you had fucked me any differently I would have evaporated into the air."

"Fucked?" exclaimed Harris. "I didn't know you knew that word. I am amazed."

"We use it all the time at the ranch. When you are working with people who speak a minimum of English, you can't use fancy phases. Short specific words are what work best."

She paused and looked into his eyes and continued, "Harris, all I have thought about all day, was your making love to me. If you had done it any other way, I might have raped you."

"Good Lord!" he exclaimed. "I pray you never have to do that."

"I thought dinner would never be over, as lovely an evening as it was," said Kathleen.

"There was no way to have chilled champagne ready for us so I guess we'll have to do with plain white wine."

"I really don't care if we have any wine right this minute or not, I want you in me," pleaded Kathleen.

Harris wasted no time filling her need completely. "You are in so deep I think your member is against my womb. Maybe it could tell my womb to open up so I can give you a son."

Harris paused. "Kathleen as much as I love you, if you conceive, I would live in mortal terror of your giving birth."

"Because of your mother?" she asked.

"That and the fact that Sophie died in childbirth."

"Oh, I didn't know why your wife died."

"That's why Maggie is raising Annie. Tommy was one month old and she was still feeding him, so the minute Annie was born she took Annie into her arms. When it became obvious that Sophie was dying, Maggie just put Annie to her breast and fed both of them."

Kathleen was silent for a long time. "If we marry will we take Annie to rear?" asked Kathleen.

"I have no idea that Maggie will ever let anyone else take care of her," stated Harris.

"She is your daughter."

"Yes, and I would love to have a son by you, but I will insist we are married by a priest if that time comes. He took her in his arms and asked, "Has the 't' become an 's'?""

"Soon, maybe soon, but I want to be in your bed every night that you will have me." said Kathleen.

"I want you in my bed every day and morning, noon and night."

"If you stay in Denver, won't you have to go to work every day?"

"I'll work out something with Tom. I'll tell him we are still on our honeymoon. Next summer I want to take you to Rome for our real honeymoon."

"Rome, oh that would be wonderful," said Kathleen.

"Of course, we will have to be legally married. You know how those Italian Catholics are. Not like the French."

"Are you using Rome to bribe me into marrying you?" she asked.

"Could be."

CHAPTER SEVEN

All Hope Dies

The next morning Harris and Kathleen arrived at Dr. Murphy's to check on the possibility of having children. When the examination was finished, Dr, Murphy talked privately to Harris. "There is certainly no question about your ability to sire a child. We have the proof already. I suggest you give her vagina a rest. It shows signs of heavy use. The fact she hasn't conceived is certainly not your fault."

Dr. Murphy continued, "Harris, her womb is tipped in such a way that no sperm can get to the opening. In some of the new medical journals, several doctors have told of a unique position some couples have used that has been successful. The women were thought to be barren."

"What is it?" pleaded Harris.

"When you and Kathleen are serious about having a child, I will tell you both. I don't want it used in the heat of passion. By the way, why does she have all those scars on her legs?"

"They are from where Fred whipped her with his belt when he found out she could not have children."

"I never liked that son-of-a-bitch to start with," was Dr. Murphys emphatic response.

CHAPTER EIGHT

Meeting the family

"It's supper time, let's go to the dining room, so I can introduce you to my Mexican family," said Kathleen.

Everyone stood up and applauded when they entered the room. Harris was accepted as a family member.

That evening Kathleen and Harris sat on the front porch of the house and were serenaded until late in the evening. Maria came up and handed each of them a candle. "To find your way to separate bed rooms." Then she winked and said, "Eyes will be watching."

They dutifully lighted the candles and went to separate bedrooms. After the entire ranch became quiet, Kathleen came down the stairs as quietly as possible, positioned herself in the doorway of the downstairs bedroom and said, "New in town sailor?"

Harris said, "Yes, but the love of my life is in the room just above us. I wouldn't want her to know."

"I'll never tell a soul," said Kathleen as she crawled into his bed.

After their lovemaking session ended they went to the kitchen to get a much needed drink of water. Kathleen said, "Tomorrow why don't we saddle some horses and ride up to half way cabin? It is a cabin Fred had renovated and one of the shepherds meets his wife for a weekend, everyone take turns."

Maria quietly entered the kitchen as Kathleen continued, "It was a considerate thing for him to do, as anything, it was intended to keep the men off the sheep and off each other. Fred also brought some board games and cards, but they are never used. Maria and I go up every Monday and gather up the linens and dust the place. The board games have never been disturbed. We dust them every Monday morning."

"Why don't you have the wife that is going up take the linens and bring them back down?" he asked.

"We thought of that, of course, but Maria and I like to have time away from listening ears."

"In the morning, Carlos and several of the ranch hands are going to take you on a tour of the entire ranch," said Maria.

"We will have to see the cabin another time," said Kathleen.

"I had wondered if I was ever going to get to see all of this place," quipped Harris.

"That will be tomorrow," said Maria.

"Great!" he exclaimed.

"Might be or not," was her reply.

CHAPTER NINE

The "T" becomes an "S"

When the touring party returned around noon, Kathleen was standing on the front porch with a big smile on her face. Harris felt there was good news about something. "Come upstairs with me," she said.

"You can't wait until tonight?" teased Harris.

"Not for this news. Do you still want to marry me?"

"More than anything," was his answer.

"Then the 'T' has turned into an 'S' and I am ready.

Harris picked her up, swung her around and kissed her heartily. "You missed me so much this morning you realized you couldn't live without me?" he asked.

"I realized that a long time ago, I can now be legally married to you."

"You have been a widow three years. What has been the problem?"

"Fred's will states that, when he dies, the children and I can live here, and they are to take good care of me and the ranch. If I remarried, I would then give up all claim to the ranch. So, I borrowed enough money from my trust fund, and bought the ranch from Fred's estate."

"Wow! You mean you are an heiress?"

"Well, yes."

"That means I can't marry you," said Harris with a smile on his face.

"Why?"

"People will say I married you for your money."

"Oh, you must be kidding me!" said Kathleen.

"No. People in town think I am just the head accountant."

"What are you?" inquired Kathleen.

"I own one fourth of the mine. So I am worth five million dollars."

Kathleen gasped. "Are you telling me the mine is worth twenty million dollars?"

"Yes."

"Now you are the one who must be kidding. There is not twenty million dollars in the whole world."

"Yes, that is what the assayers decided. Believe it or not, you are marrying a wealthy man."

"Why did they give you a fourth of the mine?"

"That's a long story for after we are married," was the only answer he would give her. Harris went to his coat and got out a small box. He opened it and got down on one knee and asked her to marry him. Of course she said "Yes."

"When did you buy the ring?" which was the largest diamond she had ever seen.

"I bought it when I bought the necklace. Jacque said I could bring the ring back, not the necklace."

"Exactly when did you buy them?" asked Kathleen.

"The afternoon after the picnic," he admitted. "When did you decide to buy the ranch from the estate?"

She replied, "The day after I slept with you the first time."

"So that was what the 'Yet' was about?" asked Harris.

"I didn't know if it would be possible or not."

"What if it hadn't been?"

"I guess we would have to live in sin. After making love with you, I was ruined from ever being with another man."

"That's a great compliment," said Harris.

"It's the truth," Kathleen responded.

"Let's get up early in the morning and go to noon mass at Andrew's. I'll ask father Roberts to marry us after mass next Sunday. If that's all right with you?"

"Are you sure you want to marry me?" asked Kathleen.

"More than anything in the world."

CHAPTER TEN

Get me to a church on time

Kathleen was sitting on the back row while Harris was in the confessional. A few minutes later, Harris came out of the confessional looking like a storm cloud that was gathering over the Rockies. He grabbed Kathleen by the hand, and all but dragged her out the church door. He was so mad he couldn't talk and helped Kathleen into the carriage and then jumped into the carriage and gave the horses a quick slap with the whip and they took off at record speed. He headed out of town, the opposite direction from the house. Kathleen was very uneasy, but sensed she shouldn't say anything. They arrived at the Harwells and he helped Kathleen step down and then went through the front door of the house like a storm blowing in.

"What a nice surprise!" chimed Maggie. "Mildred has prepared one of her famous beef roasts, and you all are just in time."

Harris' face had lost little of its anger, and all he could do was sputter out parts of words. "Maggie, bring a bottle of whisky and three shot glasses," said Tom.

Kathleen shook her head "no," but softly said, "I would like some wine."

"Certainly," said Maggie.

Tom asked Kathleen, "Do you have any idea why Harris is so upset?"

"No, he was in the confessional, and was to ask Father to marry us next Sunday."

Harris spurted out, "That hypocritical son-of-a-bitch has no right to deny us the marriage rites under any condition."

By that time two glasses of whiskey had been consumed. "Slow down, cowboy, tell us what happened." Harris ignored him and drank another shot of whiskey. "Father said he would marry us only if between right that minute, I would not touch Kathleen in any way, for a week. I couldn't even offer her my hand to get into the carriage."

"That's taking chastity a shade too far," said Tom. "I wonder how many of those bridal couples who stand before him are virgins? Not many I bet."

"I think he is punishing you for not going back to the monastery," said Maggie.

"I have seen Father Roberts slipping out the private back door at Miss Laura's on more than one occasion."

Kathleen gave him a strange look as if to say, "Recently?"

"That was back in my Lovely Rachel days," explained Harris who reached for the bottle again.

Tom stopped him, "If you drink any more you are going to vomit all over Maggie's new Persian rug. Then you will see what anger can really look like. Kathleen, take that boy up stairs and give him a massage on both sides. Use one of those back bedrooms, so any noise won't wake the babies."

"You are being crude," scolded Maggie.

"Everyone here is not a virgin. All of us have been married," retorted Tom.

Kathleen helped Harris to his feet and all but dragged him upstairs. They went into the back bedroom, and Kathleen made Harris strip all but his underpants and lie face down on the bed. Kathleen took all her clothes off except her under panties. She then straddled the small of Harris' back and started massaging his neck, The muscles were tied up in knots.

She spent a lot of time working on his neck, then moved her hands to his shoulders that were almost as tight as his neck, then she started massaging both his arms and finally stretched out her arms over his, as far as they would go. As her warm breasts touched his back Harris let out a long sigh and was asleep immediately.

Kathleen then went downstairs and Maggie prepared her a plate of roast beef and mashed potatoes. She had not eaten anything that day in preparation for taking communion.

Several hours later Harris came downstairs looking rested and refreshed. Harris looked so much like his father it almost caused Maggie to faint again.

"Harris, after you eat I have a plan that will solve all your problems," said Tom.

"I'll eat fast. I am eager to hear."

Tom spoke authoritatively, "You have to have a marriage license to keep the State of Colorado happy, so go to the Courthouse in the morning and get your license, and while you are there get married by a Judge. That will put an end to that illegal fortification."

"Don't be crude," chided Maggie. "There are no virgins here. We all know the score."

"But I want to be married in the church," said Kathleen.

"There is nothing that says you can't be married twice, and the idiot at St. Andrews isn't the only priest in the world. Can't the priest at the Spanish mission marry you? Would confessing to him be a problem?" asked Tom.

"No, I can confess in Latin" said Harris. "I have been confessing in Latin for the past ten months."

"Did you have time to learn new Latin words?" teased Tom. "You ought to be about through with the big stuff."

A strange look came over Harris' face. Then it faded quickly as his mind came back to the present. "The priest has to know Latin, or he cannot be ordained. At least he knows the Latin Mass."

"I know enough Spanish words to get by without going into details," added Kathleen.

"Well then," said Harris. "Let's do it. Maybe the priest at the mission could marry us on Sunday after the Mass. I'll go ask him tomorrow, or Tuesday as we need to check in with Dr. Murphy on Monday afternoon."

"Any change of an offspring?" asked Maggie.

"Not yet, but with a new husband we hope, especially one with a magic wand," teased Harris.

"The actual question is 'no' I am sorry to say," said Kathleen.

Quickly changing the subject Maggie said, "We'll take care of the reception plus the decorations at the mission."

"Oh, you do so much for us. I can get Maria to do that," said Kathleen.

"Sweet child," cooed Maggie. "Tom and I were married at an

army fort in Indian Territory. I would love nothing more than to decorate the church for my daughter."

Kathleen hugged Maggie. "Marrying at the mission means my Mexican family can attend," beamed Kathleen.

CHAPTER ELEVEN

The Wedding

Maggie more than decorated the mission church. She used so many candles one would have thought it was a cathedral. She had bunches of flowers tied to the end of each pew.

Later when Kathleen was profuse in her praise, Maggie said," I couldn't have been happier to do it. Like I said, Tom and I got married by the post Chaplain at a military fort. I have no daughter, except for you, and who knows, I may not live long enough to see Annie get married. So, this is the one wedding I got to help plan."

When the last candle had burned out all the guests were gone and the Harwells bid good night, the time came for the bride and groom to retire to the marriage chamber. Harris carried her upstairs and managed not trip in the dark. She lighted a lamp and when Harris saw the bed he said, "Oh dear, I've never made love on a feather bed."

"Neither have I," said Kathleen.

"How is that possible?"

"I hated the mattress Fred had on the bed, and what he did

to me on it. So the week after he died I had several of the ranch hands load the mattress on a flatbed and I took it and some kerosene and drove east until it was almost Kansas, and the trees stopped. I soaked the mattress with kerosene and struck a match, and sat on a big rock and watched it burn until dawn."

Harris took her in his arms and hugged her and said, "He really wounded you, didn't he?"

"That act came from a place of deep pain. No one on the ranch said a word about it. They understood."

"Are you ready to try it out?" Harris asked.

"More than anything, but since we are double married I want to ask you something."

"What?"

"Tell me about Tommy."

"Tommy who?"

"Tommy Harwell."

"What about Tommy Harwell?" Harris replied.

"He is your son, isn't he?"

Harris' silence had the same effect that followed a deafening thunder clap that had exploded immediately overhead. He finally inquired, "Did Maggie tell you he is?"

"No."

"Then how did you know?"

"I guessed."

"But he looks a lot like Maggie," stated Harris.

"Yes. The night she asked me if I would help her put the babies to bed, I saw her change his diaper. When I saw his male parts I knew that only one man could have sired him," explained Kathleen. "Does Tom know?"

"He is the one who suggested and arranged for it to happen."

"Why?"

"Tom is fifteen years older than Maggie, and he wanted an heir to inherit his very large estate."

"I'm surprised he didn't leave it to you," she said.

"He had already taken care of me, and it isn't the same as having a blood heir, even if the blood line was actually just from Maggie."

"So she was obviously a willing participant."

"Oh, yes," Harris said without hesitation. "She knew how much Tom wanted an heir, and she would jump off a cliff if he asked her to because she really loves him. You see, when Tom was a very young man, he was married for about thirty minutes, just long enough to get his wife pregnant. She wanted to remain a virgin, however."

"Stupid girl," commented Kathleen.

"Tom left for Kansas that night, and was in disbelief nine months later to find out he was going go be a father. He got back to Iowa just as the baby was being born. It was a boy and lived only a few hours. Tom never got over it. The family wouldn't let him see the mother nor the baby"

"How sad."

"Tom returned to Kansas and caught the mumps but would not stay in bed. He was very sick and the mumps dropped and made him sterile. We talked it over with Dr. Murphy, knowing he would never even hint at it."

"He understood the logic."

"Tom was originally a lawyer and a Judge, so he wrote up all the legal documents and Dr. Murphy witnessed all of us signing the official papers. One major stipulation was that I would have no parental rights to the child or his inheritance. Tom then locked the papers in his private vault at the bank. They were never to be made public even when he died."

"That explains a remark Maggie made the first time I sat next to her at Alfred's. She said you were a marvelous lover and then she caught herself and said, at least that's what they say on the street. I wondered what street she was talking about. I assumed Lovely Rachel would not talk. How did you get away with the tryst?"

"We had an elaborate plan that I would be seen in every bar and grill on Main Street and stay quite late. However, on the morning of the proposed event, a blizzard hit Denver, the like that even the old timers had never seen. It was a complete whiteout. I wore light colored pants and a light colored parka, not that it made any difference. Someone looking out the window would only see a shadow of a figure in the snow fall. Identifying anyone would be impossible. I followed the original plan that meant I went down to the end of the block, turned left and then took the alley behind the houses. I struggled down the alley trying to stay upright in the sheets of snow that were unrelenting in the nonstop gale force winds. I finally go to the Harwells root cellar door. It took all my strength to open it against the elements of the weather. I finally got inside and Maggie opened the door into the house. The rush of warm air was all that saved me."

"You risked your life to help them, but Tom and Maggie have household help. Surely they knew what was happening," Kathleen inquired.

"Fortunately, Jose and Matilde had already gone home or they would have been snowbound there. I felt like a frozen block of ice. Matilde had prepared a big pot of chile and another one of venison stew. Maggie had a large pot of coffee ready and many cups later as I was huddled by a roaring fireplace, I rejoined the human race. It was evening before I felt capable of fulfilling my assignment."

"Where was Tom?" Kathleen asked.

"He was at Horace Tabor's for an all-night poker game that turned into two days because of the blizzard. I'm not trying to be vulgar but our one night stand, get Maggie pregnant tryst became a two day endurance contest. It had been so long since Tom had been able to perform his husbandly duties so Maggie was sex starved. And she took advantage of my ability to fulfill her needs. Not that I minded; it was just all very tiring. If she hadn't conceived a child during those days and night she would never be able to conceive."

Kathleen interrupted the narrative, and asked, "What if she didn't?"

"It was never discussed. Tom and Maggie had a firm belief that I could accomplish the task. And I did."

Harris continued, "Nine months later Tom sent me a cable about Tommy's birth while Sophie and I were in France."

"You and Sophie were married at the time of the tryst?"

"Oh, no! If we are going to consummate this marriage that's a story for another night, and I hope you'll stay married to me after you hear the rest of it."

"Unless you have murdered someone," Kathleen said. Harris's face drained of color.

"Not with a gun," he muttered. Harris took Kathleen into his arms and held her very close. Of course, he wanted to officially consummate his marriage, but he dreaded telling her the story that he must tell her, and she could well leave him because of it.

"Kathleen, there was more to getting the five million, than just getting Maggie pregnant," Harris said dreading what came next. "I had to marry someone a week after the tryst."

"Why?" she asked.

"There had to be gossip around town that since the mining office was in Harwell's house, that Maggie and I had too much opportunity to 'carry on', as the gossips told it."

"That's ridiculous."

"I know, but I did have the reputation as a womanizer. So Tom didn't want to give anyone a chance to say the baby was mine. I had been escorting several young ladies around town, so I decided that Sophie was cute, pretty, and good company so I asked her to marry me. She was delighted although surprised and said yes."

Harris paused, then continued, "We were married the next Sunday. On Friday night I took her upstairs and seduced her. I made her believe that was why people got engaged, to try out each other's body part to see if they were compatible."

"She believed you? But you said she was a small woman and shall we say you are ample."

"Yes, but I could insert enough to give her pleasure and far enough for me to get a release," he explained.

"What did she think about that?"

"She said she was going to enjoy being married and made me promise we would do it every night."

Kathleen was laughing. "Only once a night?"

"The only problem was that the next morning her monthly flow had started early, and she was sure there was something wrong, or it was punishment since we weren't married. Dr.

Murphy assured her all was well and backed up my statement about engagements."

Harris continued, "We married the next Sunday. Sophie didn't know I was not in good standing with the church, so I did a very brief confession and took communion, which was just another act of deception. Tom and Maggie had a huge brunch following the service. Sophie was an orphan and had been reared by her grandmother, who was part of that generation that believed, that if you don't mention sex it doesn't exist. It was amazing that Sophie liked intercourse so much."

Kathleen gave a slight nod of disbelief and amazement as he continued. "We left Denver on the evening train. We had a private compartment. Sophie teared up when there appeared to be no bed. I told her the beds folded out from the wall. We went to the dining car and when we got back to the compartment the bed had been unfolded, but she was upset because it wasn't a double bed. I told her I would take the upper berth and I would come down the ladder to keep my nightly promise. Being Catholic I knew she would not approve of using anything to block conception. So on the night I seduced her, I used protection and planned to keep up that ruse as long as possible. I had no desire to drag a woman around France in her early pregnancy, and I assumed it was just a matter of hours before she would conceive. Having the top berth meant that when I came down the ladder I was ready with protection on. I always made sure the lights were off. We got to Kansas City and spent several days there shopping for clothes for Sophie. She had never been outside the city limits of Denver, so everything was a marvel to her. Then we went to New York City and we both had a great time going to the theater, and dining in famous restaurants."

"Sounds like you were having a wonderful time," Kathleen said.

"We were. One day we were out shopping, and Sophie saw a store that sold French lingerie. She had no idea what was meant by French lingerie, but since we were going to France she thought she should have some. I gave her two hundred dollars, and I went down the block to a cigar store where I bought a dozen Cuban cigars. I met her an hour later as we had planned. She came out of the store giggling with a bag hanging from each finger, and she wanted to model for me what she bought. We went back to the hotel where she did model all the lingerie, which was risqué, of course. I am a man and reacted as a man. I took her to bed immediately, sans protection. It was in the middle of the afternoon, so there was no way to use protection without her knowing it. And I realized what the consequences might be."

Kathleen asked, "Couldn't she tell the difference?"

"She did say that was the best of all the other times we made love. The next day we set sail out of New York and the first couple of days she was sea sick, but after she got used to the rocking of the boat it cleared up. Our private compartment on the ship had a double bed which pleased Sophie to no end, and I pleased her as often as possible."

Kathleen grinned as he continued, "We docked at Southhampton, and then took the ferry across to France. I rented a horse and carriage so we could go where we pleased, and stop along the way. I had travelled extensively when I was in France touring mining operations. France is a beautiful country and it was good to see it again. Paris was completely different. It had not changed all that much, but I saw the city through

Sophie's eyes, and it was like seeing Paris for the first time. The city had a sparkle I had not seen the first time."

"Did you have a chance to visit the whore you had liked so much?" Kathleen teased.

"Absolutely not! I have done a lot of things I am not proud of, but I never broke a marriage vow." Harris said seriously.

"No offense was intended," replied Kathleen.

"We stayed in Paris for ten days. One day we went to Notre Dame for the noon Mass. Of course, I was out of the Church, which Sophie had figured out, and I had confirmed. When she came back to the pew after receiving the Host, she had tears running down her cheeks. I was so moved, I immediately found a priest who was taking confessions and confessed briefly."

"It didn't take long? Did it?" asked Kathleen.

"Not like it did the ten months at the monastery. The priests there left no sin unexamined. At one point I confessed that I had cheated on an eighth grade math test."

"You are exaggerating aren't you?" teased Kathleen.

"No, you have no idea how serious those priests are about sin, and stamping it out. It took four priests to get through all of my sin. The first were two young priests who got over excited. They entered the monastery when they were fifteen or sixteen and knew nothing of the world. They were replaced by two, much older priests and finally, Father Abbott who took over as my confessor. That's when we got to the eighth grade math test. Father Abbott entered the monastery in his mid-thirties after his wife died. They had no children.

After I had done the quick confession, I went to the altar and received the Host. When I got back to the pew, Sophie had the biggest smile on her face. She was overjoyed and whispered in my ear that she had been praying for my soul every day. After we left Paris, we travelled south to the area known as the Riviera, to a resort where clothes are optional."

Kathleen gasped. "You are teasing now."

"No, I am not, and Sophie was horrified at first. The clerks at the front desk and the waiters in the dining room were clothed, some of the guests were clothed and some not, mostly not. We had our meals in our room."

He continued, "Our room, as all the others, had been carved out of rock and the floor was sand. The walls of the room were extended at least thirty feet out into the ocean which provided privacy to whomever was in the next room. Sophie did not know how to swim, so I taught her. She took to water like the Proverbial duck to water. She loved it. She said that she had never had so much fun. She spent most of the time swimming, and was sad when the tide went out."

"At that point I radioed Tom, and asked him to build a swimming pool at my house, and told him how to build on the crest of the hill and how to heat it. He didn't think it could be done. I had to remind him that I had a degree in engineering."

"Wait a minute," interrupter Kathleen. "You had fallen in love with her!"

"I guess so," acknowledged Harris.

"Guess so, my foot," exclaimed Kathleen. "No one radios half way across the world to ask a friend to build a swimming pool unless he is in love."

"Maybe the pool was a sort of repentance for marrying her without loving her. We stayed there about a week and then we drove on down to Marseilles, turned in the horse and carriage and boarded the ship to take us home. Sophie had been a little draggy which I thought maybe she was just tired, and had worn herself out swimming so much. The first day out at sea, she was so sick, I had the doctor come. After examining Sophie he said, "Congratulations Papa."

After the doctor left our cabin, Sophie asked, "Why did he call you, Papa?"

"Because you are going to have a baby. I am going to be a father."

"How can that be?" she asked. "I just stared at her. Surely she knew how babies were made, but apparently she did not."

"We have not been married very long," she said. "I didn't think babies came until a couple had been married a while."

"I decided she must have had a lot of Protestant friends. I explained to her which body parts created a baby, and how. She found it fascinating."

"You mean I could have conceived a baby on our wedding night?"

"Yes, was my answer. I wasn't about to get into using protection during intercourse, against the Church's teachings. She honestly believed that God gave you a baby when He thought it was the right time to have one. Her ignorance wasn't her fault."

"I never heard that from the nuns in my school," exhaled Kathleen.

Haris said, "When I was a senior in high school, Father Leo called all the senior boys in to explain to us what that dangly thing we had on our bodies was good for, besides urinating. He said that when we married a Catholic girl, that on our wedding night we would discover what other purpose it has. The implication was that the magic it had wouldn't work with a Protestant girl."

Kathleen was roaring with laughter and said, "You have just made all of that up."

"No, but the older boys told us, and we were all eager to try it. We could not get the senior girls to cooperate. The nuns had put the fear of hell into them, and had been more detailed in their explanation."

Continuing about his marriage Harris said, "It was a very rough crossing and Sophie was really not doing well, although she was delighted to know she was going to be a mother. She still considered it a miracle."

Kathleen smiled knowing how happy she would be to have his child.

"We disembarked at New Orleans and stayed about two weeks hoping it would give Sophie a chance to recover from the crossing. We stayed at a hotel near Jackson Square and went to Mass every day and that was about all. Then we took a steam boat up the Mississippi to the Arkansas River and got off at Fort Smith, Arkansas."

"Did you try to make connections with anyone at St. Scholastica?" asked Kathleen.

"No, and much as I would have liked to do that, I was in a hurry to get Sophie home. We caught a train at Fort Smith, changed trains at Tulsa and then it was a straight shot to Denver. Sophie was surprised that there were not Indians all over the place, running wild, since this was Indian Territory. I never mentioned that sometimes trains get robbed. I didn't want her to get so nervous she'd have the baby on the train."

"I wired ahead to Tom and Maggie and they and Dr. Murphy met us at the station. Tom had grown a mustache while we were gone. He looked as if he had been plucked up from a Board Room in a major city in the East and placed in Colorado. Brocade vest and all. His posture was still as rigid as if he were standing at attention. A trait left over from his army days.

"When we walked into our house, Sophie said, 'I don't remember those French doors at the end of the living room.' She squealed with delight when she opened the doors and saw the swimming pool."

"Dr. Murphy examined Sophie and told me the baby was very large for a woman her size. He didn't foresee an easy delivery. A few days later, I had Maggie come over and talk to Sophie about the birthing process, what to expect, etc. About ten days later Sophie went into labor, and I had Ruis take a horse and buggy and go fetch Maggie and the doctor."

"Fetch?" questioned Kathleen.

"I guess there is still some Arkansas in me. It was not an easy labor and lasted for thirty hours, but finally she was delivered, an eight pound baby girl. Sophie asked that we name the baby Sophie Anne and call her Annie. I immediately agreed."

Harris lowered his voice, "We were so excited about the baby until Dr. Murphy looked at me and frowned. He couldn't get the bleeding to stop, despite the fact he did everything he knew to do. He said that I should send for a priest, and Father gave her the last rites. Sophie understood what was happening. I pleaded with her not to die. We said the Rosary together, and I told her that I loved her."

She said, "I know you didn't love me when we married, but I know you do now. That is what matters."

"I sat by her bed side and held her hand. She squeezed my hand and said, 'Thank you for the most wonderful year of my life.' Then she closed her eyes and was gone. I broke down in uncontrollable sobbing. I was sorry to see her die, but I was also overwhelmed with guilt and the deceptions. I felt that my greed had killed her. Tom saw to it that I got drunk. The minute she was born, Maggie put Annie to her breast which Annie took to readily. Maggie was still nursing Tommy. Tom spent the night with me. He was fearful that I might commit suicide, and he was going to see to it I did not. Turns out he had good reason to be concerned."

"The funeral mass was at All Saints. At the burial, when I saw the coffin being lowered into her grave, I completely fell apart and passed out. Tom put me and a case of whiskey into his carriage and we headed south. He made sure I stayed drunk for two days, When we reached Trinidad we stayed at a lodge there and Tom poured coffee and juice down me for two days. He said I had to be completely sober before we could try to go down the road/trail that took us down and over the seven thousand foot drop into New Mexico. There were donkeys especially trained to carry people down the rugged pass. I found the trip down the path to be nerve racking, Tom being an old cavalryman sat better in the saddle than I did."

"When was Tom in the Cavalry?" asked Kathleen.

"He was the commanding General of the 13th Kansas during the Civil War. That's the group my father was in."

"So, Tom knew your father?"

"Yes, and he told me my father was killed at the end of the war in the battle of Van Buren, Arkansas. After we had reached solid ground, we went about one hundred and fifty miles and passed by Santa Fe to the Benedictine Monastery which was about twenty miles the other side of Santa Fe. Tom had wired ahead and Father Abbott was expecting us. Tom took me inside and one of the monks showed us to my very small room. I lay face down on the bed and slept for two days. I was never told, but I imagine Tom made a sizeable contribution to the monastery, and left the rest of the whiskey with the monks."

"Sort of like the Good Samaritan?" commented Kathleen.

"I suppose so," replied Harris.

"I was aware most of the times when a Brother brought a tray of food into my cell, as they call them. On the third day I drank some coffee and some broth. Later in the afternoon I went out into the close and just sat on a bench in the sunshine. I listened to the Brothers sing the Mass, and after their supper they sang Evening Praise. It was very comforting, but I sat there well into the evening and watched the stars. When desert chill descended, I went back to my room, which had been cleaned up with fresh linens on the bed and a vase of flowers on the small table. Then the next morning I went to morning Matins but just listened. I ate a light breakfast with the Brothers and then told Father Abbott I would like to start confessing, which ended up lasting ten months. I think one of the reasons Father Abbott had me come home was because I was out of new sins."

"Father wrote Tom, unbeknownst to me. Father said I was conflicted about my parents and asked if Tom could help with that when I got back to Denver. Turns out, Tom and Maggie had introduced my mother, Carolyn, to my father. The Harwells felt responsible for everything else because John had asked Carolyn to marry him. He appeared to really love her. But he found out she was a Confederate spy and had betrayed his Federal unit, plus she was with child. It was more than my father could take, and he rode out of town and shot himself in the head. He is buried at Van Buren, Arkansas. My mother went across the

Arkansas River to have the baby at her grandmother's. She died giving birth to me and the Harris family put out the word that I had died. Tom investigated and found out I was very much alive. When my grandmother died, Tom came and got me and I was turned over to the nuns at Shoal Creek. The source of the money I received was my father's estate. His family owned a foundry up North. Both parents had died about the time the war started. John was their only child so he inherited their money. Early on in the war my father had asked Tom to take care of his inheritance should he not make it through the war. Tom set up the trust fund and was the manager of the trust."

"What a tragic outcome for your parents. So, Tom was the mysterious benefactor administering your father's estate. Why was he always so insistent that you go to Catholic Schools?" she asked.

"Would you believe Tom is a baptized Catholic?"

"Really?"

"Yes, really."

"I didn't think he believed in anybody but himself," stated Kathleen.

"That is basically true. After his first wife, Eleanor, got an annulment, Tom left the church. He respects the institution of the church, but not its teachings. He has always thought the Catholic Church had the best schools. My father was a Catholic and Tom wanted me to be reared the way John McGinty would have done it"

"How could Eleanor get an annulment if she had birthed a child?"

"Eleanor claimed she was raped, and the child was the

product of the rape. She was sure the Lord would restore her virginity. She ended up going to a convent in Indiana."

"Good Lord! When will the Church get around to accepting the fact that people have sex, and stop keeping everyone so ignorant. There is nothing evil about the human body. It was created by God," exclaimed Kathleen. "If Tom didn't tell you about your father's suicide, how did you find out?"

"Before Father Abbott went to the monastery, his name was Chester Smiley. He was in the 13th Kansas with my father. He knew the truth from the beginning. He was there when it all happened. Tom was their commanding officer. Chester helped bury my dad. Since my father could not be buried in a church cemetery, Chester buried him where he was found. It was on an edge of a hillside where dad liked to go and sit, and look over the Arkansas River Valley. My father said it was the fairest view he had ever seen."

Kathleen gave him a soothing stroke on his arm.

"I was troubled about the suicide. The Church says it is a mortal sin and was a straight shot to Hell. I am glad I know about the suicide even though it isn't a pretty story."

"So, Tom and Maggie are still trying to keep it concealed?"

"Yes, and I am amused when Maggie says she is from some made up town in Georgia. She doesn't want me to know that she was there in Van Buren when all of that was going on and feels guilty because she was the one who introduced my parents."

CHAPTER TWELVE

Absolution received

Harris said, "Kathleen, I was always well taken care of when I was young, but I never had any money of my own. Tom hired me, paid me, and paid for my expenses in Europe but I felt it was just working for wages. I wanted more. Truthfully, I am not as virtuous as you think. I was anxious to get my hands on that much money and readily agreed to the tryst. I lusted after Maggie and the gold and would have impregnated a goat if that is what it would take to get that much gold. It was just pure greed. Now, I have played a game of concealment with Tom and Maggie because I have known the truth about my father and mother."

"Harris, truthfully, I don't know Tom and Maggie all that well but they have been willing participants in concealing the truth from you even if their motives were pure. You shouldn't feel completely responsible for the way all your lives have ended up. There is a history between your families going back to your father and mother that you knew nothing about, that shaped your life and theirs."

"Yes, but my lust for being rich and Maggie…"

Kathleen stopped him, "Remember you told me when Maggie opened the door and promptly fainted when you first arrived at their home in Denver?"

"Yes."

"It's obvious to me that Tom didn't inform her of your arrival, maybe not even about hiring you, for a reason. From the descriptions of your father, you and he look very much alike. Have you considered the possibility Maggie and your father were intimate before he died?"

Harris flinched at the thought and drew away some. "There's no way to know, but the way Father Abbott described him, I doubt it. I'm sure he was attracted to her but I'm the one who jumped at the opportunity to have her and line my pockets. If what you suggest is true, the sin of the father has passed to the son."

Kathleen began to draw Harris closer when he looked away and got quiet, but soon the silence was pierced by a low, sorrowful sobbing which unnerved Kathleen. She asked, "Harris, what is happening?"

"I have never told anyone about my desire for being willing to do anything to be wealthy and giving Maggie a child, and now I feel so overwhelmed with sin."

"Didn't Father Abbott give you absolution?"

"I never told him."

"You never told him! Why not?" she exclaimed.

"He would have said the words of absolution and I could have hoped God would forgive me, but Father Abbott would never have forgiven me. He might have let me become a monk, but he would have blocked me from becoming a priest. At that time, I wanted to become a priest more than anything."

Kathleen wanted to speak but he stopped her. "Before I met you, I had promised myself that when I went back to Pecos I would tell him, and accept whatever happened, knowing Father Abbott would have said since Tommy was conceived in sin, he would be unloved by God, and would go to Hell, because of our sin. I can't bear the thought of having Father Abbott say that out loud."

Realizing guilt put on him by the church was about to ruin this wonderful, loving man, she made Harris look at her and told him, "Harris, you married me the first time by talking directly to God to take the marriage vows. I don't know any reason I can't talk directly to God, and ask for absolution for you. The Protestants say that every man is his own priest. Surely that means women too."

"I have no problem with that, but Luther probably would not agree," he countered.

"I am not going to ask Luther, I am going to ask God." Kathleen bowed her head and prayed, "Dear Father in Heaven, please forgive any sin Harris feels he was involved in while giving a friend the gift of an heir and lusting for money. In Jesus name, Amen."

Harris took her into his arms, hugged her and said, "Kathleen, you have redeemed me! I must have been granted absolution because the heavy weight on my heart has lifted. I love you so much. Now, I can love you for all eternity."

"As I will love you."

About the Author

Mary Frances Hodges is a native of Paris, Arkansas and holds degrees in both history and English from the University of Arkansas at Fayetteville, plus a Master's degree in education. She retired after twenty years from the Rhetoric and Writing Department at the University of Arkansas at Little Rock.

Printed in the United States
By Bookmasters